WHY I LIE

WESTERN LITERATURE SERIES

MICHAEL GILLS

WHY I LIE

STORIES

▲▲ UNIVERSITY OF NEVADA PRESS
RENO & LAS VEGAS

Western Literature Series

University of Nevada Press,

Reno, Nevada 89557 USA

Manufactured in the United States
of America

Design by Carrie House

Library of Congress Cataloging-
in-Publication Data

Gills, Michael, 1960–

Why I lie : stories / Michael Gills.

p. cm. — (Western literature series)

ISBN 0-87417-514-3 (pbk.: alk. paper)

1. United States—Social life and
customs—20th century—Fiction.

2. Men—United States—Fiction.

3. Psychological fiction, American.

4. Domestic fiction, American.

I. Title. II. Series.

PS3607.I45 W48 2002

813'.6—dc21   2002000642

The paper used in this book meets
the requirements of American National
Standard for Information Sciences—
Permanence of Paper for Printed
Library Materials, ANSI Z39.48-1984.
Binding materials were selected for
strength and durability.

First Printing

11 10 09 08 07 06 05 04 03 02

5 4 3 2 1

FOR JILL, LYRA AND MOON

WORK IS PRAYER

Contents

I wish to thank my mother, Jacquelyn Treadwell Gills. Grateful acknowledgment goes to Jim, Traci, Kristi, Edith Treadwell, Marion Weldon Treadwell, my Arkansas people, and many who've breathed prayers on my behalf.

I must thank writers who've given time. Especially, I offer deep gratitude to Fred Chappell, John Clellon Holmes, Lewis Nordan, François Camoin, and Donald Hays. I count myself lucky to share friendship with Jim Clark. *Why I Lie* owes a hefty debt to Monica Miceli and Trudy McMurrin. For writing the *blue pee* out of this world, thanks to Dale Ray Phillips and Andrew Hoffmann, and to the postal clerks who put up with us.

These stories originally appeared in the following publications, for which grateful acknowledgment is given:

Arkansas Literary Forum: "Oratory"
Boulevard: "Conviction"
The Gettysburg Review: "Why I Lie"
The Greensboro Review: "Paradise"
Lynx Eye: "The Lifetime Loneliness Scale"
Nebo Literary Magazine: "Crystal City"
New York Stories: "For Everything About to Fall"
Quarterly West: "Where Words Go"
Salt Hill Journal: "Sightings"
Shenandoah: "Dance All Night"

"Paradise" also appeared in *What There Is: The Crossroads Anthology.*

"Where Words Go" also appeared in *New Stories from the South: The Year's Best* (Algonquin, 1998).

The author wishes to express heartfelt gratitude to the Utah Arts Council for its continuing support of his work.

WHY I LIE

FOR EVERYTHING ABOUT TO FALL

O. W. woke me and Jimmy up with a doe he'd hit while deadheading home from Memphis. This was August, a tough month, and he'd run the deer over on the Arkansas side, not far from the *Dog Track Hilton*, where he and Mama escaped when they weren't at each other's throats. I'd flunked out of a football scholarship that spring and was home to commit suicide, or lay bricks if the job came through. Jimmy was nineteen, a genius stutterer, looking for a ticket to wherever. "It just *stood* there," O. W. said, turning the key in the trailer padlock. "Paralyzed."

I said, "It see you coming?"

He flung up the trailer door, and out came a rush of sweet, cool air, the thing's eyes twinkling carnival red with street light. "Had to."

Jimmy said, "I–I was in a dream." He petted the animal's mule-shaped ear a few times, lifted the head, and let it fall. "But I don't remember it n–now."

The Kenworth's low idle rattled house windows up and down Willy Ray, was always getting reported for disturbing the peace.

O. W. said, "I'll make chili. Mama'll like that."

"Mama h–hates venison."

O. W. was always showing up with a hundredweight of Fig Newtons from a highway wreck, fifty-pound sacks of pancake batter, a refrigerator box full of Hershey's kisses, once.

"You honk? They'll move if you honk."

A light snapped on across the street, and Richie Grayback yelled to shut the hell up.

Jimmy said, "Hell with this. I'm going back to sleep."

"Shut up. Do this fast." O. W. drug it out into the ditch that cut across our front yard. "Skin it in the little house," he said. "I'll drop off and be back in an hour."

A smeared bag of Crystal City ice fell out from the belly slit.

"Don't wake Mama." His voice rained down from the roof-high cab, where radiant signal and danger lights blinked.

The air brakes hissed. I shook my head no, we wouldn't wake Mama.

"It's b–bullshit. People don't do this."

I said, "Shut up, Jimmy," and saw a face moon through a window across Willy Ray. "I'm the one who's fucking depressed."

I was in a dream.

"I'll kick your ass. I swear."

"Try—try."

We each took a hind leg and dragged.

The little house was built out of scrap wood in the backyard to mirror the big house we lived in, which was pretty small. It ended up storage for things that never made it to the dump: mower parts, a broken-down minibike, fake silk wreathes from the cemetery with *Son* and *Mother* and *Father* written on them. Windowless, it stood out under the bent apple trees, flanked by fermenting fruit and blackberry briar. In our backyard, spider webs stretched tree to tree, invisible as gill net. Here, hoppers, horseflies, and a scrap of phone bill were stringered up where fist-sized spiders walked on air.

Midstride, a big one wrapped around our faces. Some of it went in my mouth, tasteless, crackling like hair-sprayed hair.

"See what I g–goddamn mean?" My one brother bent down, spitting in the small light.

Out of nowhere. And I *felt* that spider come, the weight of its moving. I'll never forget that.

Jimmy tracked down a flashlight and found a lock-blade knife in the cooler where I hid beer. We neck-hung the whitetail from a head-high beam. Novembers down in Fordyce, this was our job, skinning and sawing stew meat while the men played poker and pissed and farted and lied and doctored hangovers.

"In a bean field, minding your own business, life out in front you. Cross the road and BAM. You're in Lonoke County."

My brother sliced a necklace. We started dressing. Hide swished away from meat. It was quiet work, we knew what we were doing, and Jimmy was an ace with a jackknife. One of the neighbor's rabbits was squealing—they'll do it when it's hot.

"I want out'a here." Jimmy ran the blade down one ham to the musk gland above the hoof split. "Out'a this house. Out'a this t–town. Out'a p–pissant Arkansas. I don't even like my name. Get me out'a it, too."

Skinning an animal is not unlike taking off a glove. Saw a line down the spine, quarter, and bone. "That's stupid, Jimmy. What's someone do without a name. How'd you order checks? Or get married? What would your kids say on first day of school? Hi, I'm nobody. Glad to meet you. Hey, ever'body, meet my brother, no-body."

"I hate August. Is it anywhere n–not August."

He put the blade between his lips and we yanked down hard, the soft skin hooked in our fists so a vertebra in the neck cracked. We were almost home. One ham bone snapped from the inner socket. The meat wouldn't smell for a while. I laid it out in the grass under the crooked apple while Jimmy went at the other.

"L–look at us." He stepped back for a second, and we took stock.

Lit by flashlight, the minibike's broken headlight hung on a red wire, a panful of black motor oil floated crickets, and the deer head's blood leaked watery on fake flowers. Jimmy was nineteen. I was twenty-one.

"Go to school."

"Right."

"Any peckerhead can get a student loan. Lay it in the bank. Party ever' night."

"Yeah. Eee–easy."

"Beats hell out laying bricks. You're smart. I'd go to school."

"You already did, bub. We're not school kind'a people."

My hand printed his shoulder. I said, "Don't you tell me what I did. Got me?"

Cop car lights swirled through the space between our houses, a neon shine in the web we'd half knocked down. Jimmy went first. An idiot siren-bleeped once, again. In our front yard, a deputy was shining his door spotlight on the bloody ice bag, following the trail we'd dragged across the burnt-up grass.

"Evening boys." His window opened just a little. "What's all this here?"

It was Simpkins. He'd been here before. Back in high school, he was a fat boy with asthma whose father ran the funeral parlor where jewelry disappeared. Now, he wore a gun and knew every black mark on your record from here to kingdom come. He knew that I'd lost my scholarship at the university, and he knew why.

Jimmy wouldn't talk. The light was hard.

"Daddy hit a deer. It's out back."

Simpkins leaned into his seat, looked at me, then Jimmy. His radio monkey-chattered. "We had some calls."

"Yeah."

The window rolled down all the way, and cool air that stank of Aqua Velva leaked out. He pushed a mag light our way, pointed it at Jimmy. "You a mess, son."

"I told you. We just cleaned a deer."

"Ain't talking to you, hoggy-boy. Talkin' to Jimbo."

I could feel eyes on us, someone watching. Mama was inside, on a bed running over with romances page-marked with razor blades, old encyclopedias, and pictures of us when we were little.

"Hey Jimmy? What's goin' on here?"

I said, "Listen, Simpkins."

"Shut up. Just shut t' fuck on up," he said, which I did. Cops, policemen, officers of the law—even the lard-assed Lonoke County kind—made me nervous. They could arrest you, lock you down, and I've never understood how someone does that.

"Now say, son. Why you all bloody?"

Jimmy said, "F–fuck off, Simpkins," turned, and walked.

The door opened, and the deputy got out. It was Arkansas humid, not long from two-a-days outside Panther Field, where I'd run for two hundred seventy-five yards one long-gone autumn night against Bauxite.

"Jimmy? Why you tell me to *f–fuck off?* You come back here now."

In my head, the loud cicadas, clapping, the Ozark hills turning gold to fall, ten thousand red-dressed Arkansans making a joyful noise. A noise soaring and falling and soaring over me as I handed over the kickoff I'd just returned and heard my name said loud into the ears of my mother and my father and my one brother. I'd lost my mouthpiece. My breath turned to feathers, and I saw light in their faces across the distance, and the world seemed like the right place to be.

"*T–talk* to me, Jimmy."

My brother just walked away. It was over, probably. But until the billy stick caught the side of my head, I threw one forearm shiver after another up under his skull. Left, right, left—it hit me that we were who we were, people who ate roadkill, whose hearts got broken early on and stayed that way. Being poor was a way of thinking, a mind-set you couldn't outrun with a suitcase full of money. It was tattooed on your brain, and you held it against your kin, against your brother even. We all of us wanted the hell out, but the game was fixed.

O. W. was making a pot of venison chili when we walked in the front door of our house. He met us just inside, wearing a flowered apron that was way too small. He waved a wooden spoon, reddened to the handle with chili powder, paprika, and cayenne.

"I was thinking you two were disappeared," he said. "And left our meat out for the dogs." He looked me straight in the face. "What got ahold of you, Jack?"

I said, "Nothing. Cops came by."

Jimmy had thought it was funny, hilarious, me and the fat lawman. "Jack knocked S–Simpkins into next week. He KO'd him."

"What for?"

My split lip oozed. At the station, Chief Self pointed out my number, forty-five, in last year's wall calendar, where a Razorback cheerleader was photographed falling into muscular arms. He gave me the talk about athletes assaulting people and released me. Jimmy signed papers.

I said, "They wondered about the deer. Nobody's killed."

Cooked venison and chili powder were thick in the air. "Good," O. W. said. "This'll cure you. What's it need?"

Floating in beer were kidney bean, jalapeño, purple onion, and tomato. Ground hunks of O. W.'s kill smelled good in the hot kitchen.

Jimmy swallowed two spoonfuls. Steam clouded his face. "Hotter," he said. "Lay in some crushed reds."

O. W. said, "Can do. I'm all for that."

The three of us tinkered over the bubbling mix, throwing in fistfuls of whatnot until we got it right. We grated cheese, diced onion garnish, and poured Tabasco until the hot rolled off our faces, down our arms, onto the chopping block.

Jimmy laid out three places at our table, opened a box of saltines, and poured buttermilk into frosty glasses. "Lord," O. W. offered, "preserve us and protect us, cause we 'bout to eat chili for breakfast. Amen."

Amen. Eat.

And that's what we did. We devastated the blistering meal while O. W. told how the road was changing, how his runs didn't pay, how he was going to buy a set of golf clubs and play his way across the country, take our mama with him. "The senior tour," he said. "We could maybe make it big. Guarantee you."

I said, "I'll go tomorrow."

"G–golf? Just what I need." Jimmy grinned a shit-eating grin and laughed some. "I can't get over you, Jack. You kept sayin', 'You had enough? You had enough?' Then he pop–popped you."

O. W. said, "It's a rich man's game. But I've won money at it."

"This's *better* than my dream. Much b–b–b–b–b—. Better than my dream."

We took seconds, thirds, drank the whole quart of milk, made

Mexican cornbread, and fed ourselves until there was nothing to do but go at it again. We stripped off our sweaty shirts and grazed.

By sunup, O. W. was slicing butterfly steaks for more breakfast. Mama walked in on us, caught us breaking the last eggs into a cracked batter bowl. She was combing her hair, long strokes down from her widow's peak. Any second, she'd choose to say or not say the thing that crossed the line.

"What's wrong?" She said it to me. "Is everyone crazy?"

Decent families up and down Willy Ray were just now rousing from sound sleeps, glimpsing the fine morning from sunny backyards, lazing into the end of a season.

"Maybe we are," O. W. said, straight-faced. "But it's *good* crazy."

"*Good* crazy? What's that supposed to mean?"

O. W. said, "Look. I'm making you breakfast."

"So what?"

That second, I watched her decide how we would remember the morning. A dusty Polaroid stayed on the fireplace mantel, a remnant of the days when it could get you to the sideline for a shot between quarters. For a reason that escapes me, she picked it up and looked at us through it.

"Sweety," O. W. said in a voice I'd never hear again, "get one of the three of us." He disappeared out the back door, came back with it in his hands. "With our trophy."

My mother gasped.

"It's hideous," she said. "Stand over yonder."

She arranged us in front of the fireplace, O. W. in the middle, Jimmy to his right, and me on the left. My brother and I each grabbed an ear as O. W. spread his arms over our shoulders. The flash caught us looking straight into the camera eye, winged beneath our old man's arms. The dead deer's tongue is pink, I see now, between its teeth. O. W. seems about to speak. Jimmy's blue, blue eyes fix and evaluate, maybe sense some kind of trouble down the road. I'm surprised at how all-American I look, like Jimmy's twin almost, believing my life over and done. The whole thing was about to fall apart. Nine months down the road, Jimmy'd miss a turn. Daddy and me, we'd find him at Conway Funeral Home. In the forever of a silver casket, his lips would be sewn shut with clear thread. *Fuck off,* he'd said. *I want out.*

"Look," Mama said. "See?"

She fanned the developing picture in front of a stiff breath. We gathered, the four of us, waiting for the rest of our lives. In my mother's hand, three morning fools, *light* in our eyes.

CONVICTION

For a while in my twenties, I worked for a contractor named Jake
Fuller and his son, Tommy, who was studying for the bar. Jake
hired me over the phone, said to bring tools. I was busted at the
time, writing hot checks, eyeing people at cash machines and
bank drive-throughs. From the first syllable, he knew that I was
white, and I knew that he wasn't. A part of me that I'd come to be
ashamed of relished the idea of a black boss, eating from a hand
my people had bitten. This, my mind, that first morning, walking
across old Highway 71, down into a woody hollow, blacktown,
where you could smell food cooking, meat, pork maybe, which is
what I remember because I was hungry. In windows, an occasional face caught, turned back light. The church I was to help out
on was built so that its broad back turned against Fayetteville,
where I'd walked from that morning. The new wing butted into
the main sanctuary's west side. I'd been taken on for inside work,
sheetrock and trim, stain and finish. Early, I wandered the

building's perimeter, deciding whether or not it would be okay to piss on the backside.

Jake caught me midstream. "You him?" His voice carried over a pile of wood scrap.

Urine leaked down my leg, at once warm and cold. "Mr. Fuller?"

"Step down here." A flurry was passing; it was January, freezing.

We shook. Fuller led me though a sheet of split visqueen, onto a concrete floor where stacks of chalky drywall leaned against studs stripped in between with paper-backed insulation. I was grateful. "What's this gonna be?"

Jake's brown eye had a trace of blood in it, near the left pupil. He was shorter than me, chunky, bull chested. "Not a place to piss on," he said.

I told him that I was sorry because I was.

Light was on from a strung-up cord, we could see fine. "A fellowship hall," he said. "Suppers, potluck, Sunday school, whatever. Poker, some nights, I imagine."

"I forgot to ask you what you pay. What do you pay?"

Jake smiled a little, then lifted the cuff of his left shirtsleeve, where a gold wristwatch glittered. "What're you worth, son?"

Rasping through the split plastic, a lighter man entered, eating a biscuit or a doughnut, I couldn't tell. "Morning, Pop."

"Tommy," Jake said, "this fellow's helping us now for a while."

Jake's son nodded, shook my hand, and I told him who I was, that I appreciated the job. A silver space heater fired up at the room's far end, one red eye hissing near the double doors that I guessed led into the main building. The smell of kerosene turned my stomach a little.

"Bathroom's through there," Jake said, guessing me. He told us that he was running up to the lumberyard and told Tommy to grab the thermos from the kitchen, which was at their house, a block or so up the street.

"You want coffee?" Tommy raised his brows.

I said, "Sure I do," and he told me that he'd be right back. Alone in the new church wing, I laid my nail apron down.

The right side of the double doors swung open freely and out came a rush of sweet warm air. Rosy light washed in through the stained-glass windows so that the place seemed a replica of where I'd been churched, down to the block letters announcing last Sunday's attendance at two hundred seventy-seven. The aisle took me to the main doors, heavy wood with brass handles and carving even. There, I looked down onto the quiet sanctuary, the wooden pews, the falling middle aisle, a pulpit centered behind an altar where a stack of silver plates were stacked beside a vase filled with yellow, red, pink—who knows what all was there—flowers. Behind the pulpit, a choir loft raised up in a semicircle in front of a baptismal like where, once, a blank-faced preacher wearing duck-hunting waders under a soaked robe held my head down until my last air was gone, by the hair of the head, so I could see the white ceiling throb and an organ tune quavered up through my gut, and it felt like some stupid trick, a joke searing through my great blind spot. Breathing hard through my mouth now, I took a few steps downward; my boots were dirty, had been peed on. Then, the image reared high on the colored wall. There, glistening above marble, a neon green cross, a blood-spattered black man hanging. His cheekbones were stripped bare to the bone, and his legs, arms, sunken-in chest were swarmed by mosquito, bottle fly, praying mantis; vultures ripped remnants of the eyeballs between razor beaks, stretching pink muscle. His hollow eye sockets rocketed through me out the wooden doors, into the frosty morning that smelled like food, like pork, like anything to put between my lips. The blue-blank eyes pinkened in the glass light, and I understood that underneath him a leering white face offered up the vinegared sponge on spear tip as the white thieves on either side cocked their heads to the shocking news that they'd walk with him today in Paradise. At the foot of the altar, against hard wood, the smell of cut flowers, of cedar, of drawn water, of the bitter embraces that had once welcomed me into the world of the just made perfect, I saw each of the silver plates was brimful with dollars, tens, twenties, a few fifties and hundreds, quarters, dimes, nickels, half dollars. I lifted my face, arrested, to eyes like moments of light that knew and knew and knew me to the crooked core. Jesus, I thought, and the altar was cold against my belly.

"Hellfire and damnation," Tommy said from the open door to my left. The thermos cup steamed. "It's hot."

And I turned to take what he offered.

In my father's house, I've heard *nigger* used as adjective, verb, and noun in the same sentence and more than once during Sunday prayer. Our two-story rent house burned down the summer that my mother and brother and me rode a Trailways bus from Arkansas out to sunny California. My father was a driver then. This was before he lost his license and our family got tickets to go wherever for free. We had people in Santa Ana—my mother's cousin Joquita—and went to stay with her to see the Pacific Ocean and Disneyland, maybe, if the money held, which it didn't. Joquita had been burned, horribly, when she was a girl, but she still got around fine, could drive with no hands even, and didn't seem the least embarrassed by her disfigured face. At the beach, on her sandy towel, while I swallowed mouthfuls of the salty water because I by god could, my mother cooked lobster red. After, back at Joquita's, she couldn't even stand the touch of a shirt, of a cotton sheet. For two days, until the burn cured, she lay in bed, just moaning, always wanting another ice cube or a sleeping pill. Joquita bought us Chinese food, which I'd never tasted before. What I remember: the sweet roughness of egg roll dipped in duck sauce; chickened rice falling through thin sticks—I ate handfuls; sour sweet pork until my stomach ached full and good; spooning stock into my mother's mouth until she said stop. People wonder why I cook.

You get to know people on the bus. The driver let me and a boy whose name won't come sing on the microphone up front. My mother shared a seat with a woman who'd ridden west on our same bus, two weeks earlier. They shared family histories, Jesus, the small things that disgusted them about men, baby pictures, shoe and bra sizes, and what they would have been if they could have chosen to be anyone on earth—Mary Kay driving a pink Cadillac, Mother Teresa, an airplane gunner—anything at all. Jimmy, my kid brother, was just starting to stutter. He was a genius, real smart, but people cocked their heads when he talked. Over the microphone, the singer-boy mocked my brother's "D–d–

d–d–d–daddy's home" down to the quiver in his jaw. I made the kid eat a dime and a nickel, a dumb thing to do. By Fort Smith, we had the same driver who'd brought us partway out. I was sitting on the step, just behind him, when he turned to my mother and her new friend and said, "It's hell, ladies, idn't it?"

"What do you mean? How so?" the women asked.

"Two weeks ago I drive you outta Little Rock, and next thing you know your house burns to the ground. A hell of a thing, and I'm right sorry."

My mother's eyes—deep brown, chestnut—teared immediately. She's tender like that—angry and beautiful and easily touched, the women who've raised me. "Lord," she said. "God. We'll do whatever we can." She was full cry now. "We have clothes and blankets and fresh tomatoes. We have a slaughter pig." She touched the woman's face, who was also crying now, with her fingers. In the rearview, the driver's face went white. I saw it happen.

"Honey," my mother's new friend said, "it ain't me."

The driver kept his mouth shut after that, so we were driven for some hours, just wondering, imagining the smell of skin, hair, teeth burning. My father met us at the terminal and held my mother for a long time under a blinking sign that said *Good-time Tulsa*. The next day, they sifted ashes with window screens borrowed from a neighbor's house, all eyes on anything. Years later, the truth would be told, my old man was pass-out drunk, cigarettes, a stove-top burner, but for then, neighbors reported seeing a black family, parked near the side of our gravel drive, picking muscadine berries.

Niggers did it, the story went, and that family was found, *punished,* my father said. They wouldn't be burning down white people's houses again, and *that buck spade would never pass his seed down to another house-burning nigger.* It's an old, old story. After, my old man held his tongue and bittered.

That night, I trapped mice behind the kitchen stove, which I used to heat my shotgun apartment. They're wild for peanut butter, and I pitched four or five out the door into the grown-over lot behind the dog food plant. It was Monday, which meant I was having pinto beans—just like Tuesday and Wednesday and Thursday—but I was thinking about writing a check to Roger's Pool Hall, where they liked me enough to file my bad notes under *F* for fiction. The truth is, what I kept rolling over in my head, was that black Jesus and the plates full of money stacked on that wooden altar. It was the epitome of too fucking much. Why in the name of Christ would people leave money out like that? What were they thinking? I didn't think of myself as a thief. I'd taken a little here and there: brown eggs and a fat bantam hen from a widow-woman's henhouse; whiskey, underwear, some socks, and a hand-saw from a man I cut hay for; a couple books, a hundred dollars, a *Penthouse* magazine from a 7-11; a piece of a tooth from a son of a bitch named Angel that I called Devil because he broke my nose; a package of hotdogs, once, cigarettes, a lot, nothing worth feeling too bad about.

We do what needs to be done.

Sheetrockers have long arms, the joke goes; carry enough and you'll believe, hear the tendons in your shoulders cluck and natter. It was snowing the next morning when I got to church, and Mr. Fuller had decided to trout-fish up near Calico Rock, where the world record German brown had been landed. Tommy'd recruited a neighbor friend of his, and the three of us were to get a good knock on the ceiling. The boss's boy was screwman, while his buddy—Tommy called him A. D., but his name was Anthony Davis—and I muscled the eight-foot boards up to the ceiling joist and tacked corners. It was hard work, really, and I could see it snowing outside, big flakes like half dollars falling and piling and falling. I've never been worth all that much in the daytime when it's snowing; some unrooted part of me wants to drink toddies, pull someone out of a ditch or something. But, mostly, I was thinking about how in my head the money was already mine.

"They fuck you," Tommy was saying. "They bend you over and fuck you hard."

We'd knocked in a few rows, staggering each board so that it split the crease in the row before. A. D. had loosened up some. Up front, we made each other nervous. "Slap, slap, slap," A. D. said. Tommy was slicing in a hole for a light fixture.

"What do you mean they fuck you?"

Tommy sliced a paper circle, knocked it out with his knife's butt end. He lowered his hands, grabbed either side of something invisible, humped air. "Like that."

A. D. said, "One time I broke down on the side of the road." He pulled the bill of his cap to the left, or maybe it was to the right— he pulled it one of those ways. "Other side'a Pine Bluff, nothin passin through the middle of nothin."

I said, "I've been there."

Tommy farted out loud. "Pardon my French," he said.

"Anyway. I got out the car. Battery's dead, and I'm automatic, and that means no go. Understand?" Sheetrock flat on top of his head, Tommy tacked his two corners, denting the paper. "And I'm standing at this crossroads. One way goes one way and the other way the other. I ain't walkin neither way. No way in goddamn hell. First car a silver something. Maybe a Cutlass. Anthony Davis stands there waving both my hands." A. D. sighted me down the rock hammer's barrel.

Tommy said, "Bang, bang, baby," and screwed sheetrock screws with a power drill every eight inches or so along the board's width and length. Our scaffold board bent, squeaked a little. "Like this, mister."

"Next car is a high shade, cream, maybe. I wave, and that little girl's eyes go big fish like this. Next?"

Tommy's face brushed mine. His aftershave smelled like medicine. "What time was it?" he asked.

"Afternoon. About three."

Tommy said, "Sharp screws," kissed a finger.

Up inches from the ceiling rafters, fumes from the space heater made you high, made your head shift gears. Still, I was there enough to hear how what they said, said many things at once, or, maybe I just needed to take a shit or something. "Why not just walk on back to town? Hire a tow truck?"

"Count to twelve. That's how many drove on by. Out in the country, and a pretty purple sun starts to set a little because it's

December and dark early. And that cold, country-ass smell that gets in your nuts. And then went a cottontail, old skinny rabbit, sliding up through the fence thicket. Only see it in pieces. Run rabbit."

We'd finished a run. Tommy let his drill down by its cord, and it came alive for a moment—just a skiff of sound—on the concrete floor. The three of us were standing on a twelve-foot two-by-ten board that swayed, bucked, cracked a little. We'd worked our way to the dark side where there were no windows. It was strange, in church, standing on a bent board, our voices disappearing in the dim air.

"You have a gun? A pistol?" Tommy was the man. We waited on him.

"What'd he need a gun for," I threw in. "To kill the rabbit?" I recalled times I'd been broken down roadside. Once, in an overheating Pontiac, I'd stopped every ten miles to take water from whatever house happened to be close. The redheaded girl with me insisted that we leave notes. I took a milk bucket from a sucked-up barn.

"How about a jump? What you needed was a jump."

A. D. said, "You the stupidest hillbilly son of a bitch I've ever seen."

Tommy laughed out his nose, said that he was hungry.

"You say my mama's a bitch?"

"Your mama? Your mama drove by me that day a dozen times and ain't quit driving yet." A. D. stepped off the scaffold, turned his back on me. "Lunch. Eat time."

"My mother never drove by you. You don't even know where I'm from. You don't know our car. Say that again."

The man stopped. "I won't." He opened one hand, held it as if offering a shake. "I won't say that, brother, again."

"Bet you won't. You better not," I said.

Outside Jake's house, a nice trilevel he'd built with his own hands, sawhorses stacked on top of each other in a tall garage where crosscut, table, and chop saws were stored, along with aluminum ladders and a real old black Corvette under a clear tarp. Tommy took us right in, sat A. D. and me at a countertop with bar stools surrounding it, asked if pasta was okay.

"Anything," I said. "I've been smelling food all day."

A. D. stripped off his coat, began to thumb a *National Geographic* from the countertop. You could hear wind shearing tree branches outside. "Goddamn monkey magazine. Monkey's ass, monkey's white teeth. Watch Mr. Red-dick Monkey use a stick to get his food." A. D. passed the open book my way. Some tribe—South American?—danced with the white anthropologist who'd suffered himself to drink a bowl full of whatever kind of whiskey was being drunk. "Ole monkey man'll dance for ya massir," A. D. said.

· The inside of the Fullers' home was like nothing I'd ever seen; everywhere was yellow, red, gold, fabric, cloth walls, feathers, shells, all lit up by bright lights hidden who knows where. Statues, totem pole faces smiled through painful grimaces in the corners; one was tall enough to look me in the eye from where I sat. Masks—shrunken heads?—eyed me from the walls, demon-looking things. To me, they were just nice to look at. If mine, they'd be hanging from my walls.

Tommy microwaved a bowl filled with spaghetti and meatballs that smelled like heaven, and a loaf of French bread was heating in the stove. He bowled up three lettuce and tomato salads, sat them in front of us with a jar of real mayonnaise.

"There's Italian if you like."

I said thanks and munched. A. D. sliced his into bite-size pieces. Half mine was down before he even chewed.

"Lord, lord. Better lay down more noodles." He removed the napkin from his lap and wiped the corner of a lip.

I look at my food when I eat, don't talk, have never really understood people who have serious conversation during supper. For me, it's serious business—get it down.

The spaghetti appeared along with a bowl of grated Romano. I dug in while Tommy and A. D. finished the breakdown story, something about how finally the car just decided to start—no problemo. It was dark, nearly, and A. D. drove to a gas station, a Phillips, and the attendant told him to get his black ass home before sundown, just like that, A. D. said.

One fat meatball tasted of fennel. Losing that hog got under my mother's skin. My parents had scraped to buy the shoat for slaughter the spring before the fire. We'd fattened it on table scraps and pellet feed, even laid out for a used chest freezer. On kill day we gorged on fresh fried backstrap, blood gravy. Over a plate of potatoes or pintos and ketchup, she'd start talking. "Think about those short ribs," she'd say, or, "Sausage S.O.S. sure would hit the spot." Other losses couldn't be so easily spoken: certain photographs, the burnt Bible, hair clipped from loved heads cushioned already in caskets. After the divorce, my father off in Florida—a place called the Space Coast—I started learning tricks with pasta. Jimmy perfected cinnamon toast, which he couldn't say without locking into the *s* sound, hard words.

"The truth, bet your ass," A. D. was saying. Tommy pushed more bread my way, recalling a man's name who'd been found nearby with his own penis cut off and stuck down his mouth, his throat.

They used real butter here. I couldn't imagine. Even my iced tea had a wedge of real lemon. Jesus.

"Walk on back to town. Just hire a tow truck, righto?" A. D. tapped his plate with a silver-clean knife, sliced a semicircle in the air near his crotch. "That's a mouthful, shine."

"Whatever," I said, and meant it. Fed, the money was burning a hole in my brain.

I brought a black girl home for Christmas dinner one year. It was something I could do. Tommy and A. D. didn't really get a kick out of this, but they hung on the story of my father's beating the head off the effigy at Central High School. The National Guard was called into Little Rock to make Governor Faubus eat crow. Everyone knew the story, some part of it. The law came down on integration, and the whole city went wacko. My mother and father were seniors that year at Central. On the day that Ernest Green and Minnie Jean Brown were ushered toward the school in the long black car, the streets were filled, packed, people on top of people, everyone, the pointy hats, the mayor, judges, the Razorback head football coach, preachers, hell-raisers, red asses, bar owners, the president of Worthen Bank, everyone up to the governor given the day off to fight the good fight against the invading Yankee feds, all hollering the rally cry, *go home, niggers, go home.*

"And your old man leadin' the parade? Cracker cheerleader?" They'd laid down their tools, it was a story. I was talking. My old man was from poor people, *poor* poor, had had to work his way through, deliver groceries, mow the man's grass, loading docks, whatever. That day he was with the toughs, seventeen-, eighteen-year-olds with a few baseball bats, some beer bottles. They were not what would be considered lowlifes or losers. They were their people's children. Anyway, a few of them had gotten together an old white shirt, some pants, and a pair of shoes. One had brought a fedora, and another stuffed rags in a pillowcase. They hung the effigy—by then it had *nigger* Magic-Markered in big letters across its chest—from the senior tree in front of the high school. The major television networks were on them, cameras rolling, waiting, asking for something to happen, zooming in on the fat markered lips, the exaggerated nose, the curly black hair that had been shaved off a cur dog. Everywhere, the air bleated with a family of voices, shouting, demanding, hallowing the sentence: *go home, niggers, go home.* Some of them, those caught up in the moment's spirit, carried crude weapons, square-point shovels, pots and pans, a few shotguns, scissors, a fishing rod rigged with lead and three razor-sharp treble hooks.

"Tell it," Tommy said. He was different. I could see the law buck up in him. A. D. sucked his teeth, looked at me the way you look at a wrecked car.

Some way my old man ended up with the baseball bat in his hands. The chant had changed. Now, the voices that had become one voice said *kill the nigger, kill the nigger* or *knock LeRoy's teeth out* or *die pickaninny,* or something like that, thousands and thousands of them, and my old man holding the bat. Cameras rolling.

Shyly at first, like he was about to offer to shake hands or ask about the weekend basketball game, he stepped up to the mock black man and swung hard chest high. In the film, the effigy bends double, bobs from the limb, *jigs,* the people would later say. Righteous applause, bigger than anything, the bare blue place where words go, the sky house come down, raining. His next swing knocks the head clean off, sends it flying, and the film gets shaky. I'm not sure what happened after that. I'd forgotten.

"What's that make you, motherfucker?" A. D. strapped on his

nail apron, thumbed the rock knife's cold, curved blade. "Why you tell that shit in my goddamn church?"

Outside, real weather had gone to drizzle. The snow was melting. No sun, no moon, dim light like you see from the bottom of a hole. "I'm just saying it happened. I'm bringing it to the table. And my old man isn't so bad. He's who he is."

"So this's supposed to help you feel good. Working with niggers?"

"Yes," I said. "No."

Tommy said, "I've *seen* that film. Man they'll fuck you up."

I looked A. D. in the face. He was taller than me, could probably kick my ass if he wanted. His skin was like a tan on someone who took the sun well, neither black nor brown nor copper nor any color exactly, but not bad to look at. It was what it was. We'd never be friends, and that was okay by me. He knew things, hat signs, gas stations, the threat of your own dick down your throat, how to eat with decent manners.

I said, "You want to cut me? Cut me."

A. D. did not suffer me a smile. "Your breed makes me want to smoke," he said. "Give me a cigarette."

So I did. Then we went back to work, sheetrocking the ceiling, in the quiet while it drizzled outside, speaking of small, stupid things, as changed as things about to disappear.

That night, a crisp twenty-dollar bill folded in my pants pocket, I walked Dickson Street, Fayetteville's mainline up to the university, a street with bars, music, and Roger's where working men drank alongside judges, lawyers, cops, thieves, and, tonight, me, whatever the hell I was. What I wanted was to get drunk, knee walking, dog-ass drunk, twenty dollars, twenty Budweisers. It had been done. This was Tuesday night, around eight, and you could hear the music playing next door—reggae—at a place called Lilly's, which Roger's folk hated. The Hogs were playing that night, basketball, and the television wired up at the end of the bar was full blare. The second half was on, and the boys were down by ten or so. Bass pulsed through the wall from next door. On television, lean black men, my age, nearly, muscles rippling, airborne, all slick-holy grace, made the motion of bodies a thing to look at, which we did. They were from Lonoke, Paris, Stuttgart, drove Porsches, Mercedes, had beautiful blonde women.

"Someone shut that nigger shit up," a red-faced man screamed down the bar. "Coon ass grows greener grass," another whooped, and someone threw in a *whoo pig, sooie.*

I ordered a Slim Jim, gave the bar back a buck, told him to keep it coming. Beside me, a clean, bearded man sat reading a book, his lips moving around shallow breaths, face mooned by the TV's brightness. "Good game," I said, chewing.

"What?"

"Close game." I guessed him my father's age.

He took a drink from his drink, sat it carefully down on the wet circle where it had been. He wore wacky reading glasses, was a university man, I imagined. Professor smart-ass come to the bar to look down his nose, to do time. I wasn't crazy about drinking beside teachers, spending stolen money.

"I know you," he said. "I've seen you."

"I don't think so."

The game was tightening. The Hogs were making a run on Memphis, sinking baseline shots, hitting in the paint. Bets were being made, money changing hands.

"You're under conviction." He spun just a little on his stool, his breath on me like fresh-dug dirt. "Aren't you?"

"How's that?" No professor, a crazy more likely, just out of Charter Vista, stoned on lithium.

Through the wall, the words were clear: *put down da books and pick up da gun, Rasta man go to Vietnam.* A billiard shooter scratched hard, the cue ball clack-rattling the long room's length. Someone screamed, "You lose."

"You just seem like someone who's out looking for something tonight. That right, bucko? You looking for something?" He grinned, touched the corner of his mouth with a pink tongue.

I downed mine, started the next, steam rising from out of the bottleneck. "I'm lost here," I said. "I'm watching the game. I'm drinking beer."

"It's written all over your face. I know what you want."

I said, "Jesus. What's wrong with you people?"

"You tell," he said, then looked at me for a second, forgot me. It was just bar talk. People could say anything, on a Tuesday night, in Roger's, during a ball game. Drunk fools, wicked people, I thought, folding what was left of my twenty. Behind me, as I walked out the glass door, its tied-on cowbell ringing, men praised and mocked, cursed and made prayer. Their voices bleated, then fell silent as the door sealed shut. Queer son of a bitch. Book readers. How could anyone know what I wanted?

To get home, it was necessary for me to walk through a cemetery, a big old graveyard that had been around as long as the city had stood. The sky had cleared, and it was bone cold. This place was rich with monuments to Fayetteville's fathers, high, white obelisks glittering under fat Ursa Major, the new moon, the goat's dim cluster. Back home, my mother and father—remarried for the third time—were no doubt rooting for shots to drop in the game I'd just walked out on. I was one of them forever, that much wouldn't change. My path wound down the hill's slight fall, to a darker place where I'd never walked but knew it led toward home. From leaf and dry grass, I stepped out onto a parking lot for an apartment building built next to Hill Street. This was the backside. Curtains were open in one of the big sliding glass doors where, inside, a woman in a gown was playing a stand-up harp. I quit walking, stood alone in the stillness. Her eyes were closed, and I could tell that she was hearing each note, willing melody, imagining what lay behind sound's invisible movement, that much I could see. After a moment, she stood, drew the curtain, and the lights went out. And I was just somebody standing in a parking lot, outside a cemetery. That was me. Still, I had seen what I had seen, the woman's fingers moving on the silver wires, pluck and quiver, the tilt of her head, the fall and bob of her shoulder, invisible music on a night splayed by Pleiades—some things were holy, if only until curtains closed. Even stars stutter. We are made of stars.

I decided to steal every red cent. Jake was there the next morning, a fine, bright Wednesday. A radio was going, the college station, classical or Spanish guitar or something, I got them mixed up. It was warm inside, the space heater purred, and Fuller was on stilts, taping off the seams at the far end of the sheetrocked ceiling. Tommy, Jake said, had a wild hair up his ass, had spent the night in the law library, and A. D. had come down with the sour stomach, cramps.

Behind me, the visqueen sounded like dead cornstalks when winter blows through, a sad sound accompanying the guitar's fretted tremolo. This was January; I was twenty-five years old, a quarter century, halfway to fifty, old enough to have been married, have children of my own, a house, a bank account with checks, a car, clean towels, someone to give a back massage to on a quiet evening after a good supper.

"You catch that game last night?"

I said, "Yessir. A little."

He was good, really, laying down a straight strip with the tape gun, crimping, flattening edges, ten feet tall on the stilts. "Our boys come back. Don't quit. That's what separates us."

I said, "That's the truth."

He looked down on me, blood still in one of the brown eyes that were the same color as my mother's—creamy, kind, capable of sudden and great anger. "You never said what you're worth, son."

I wanted to work, then, dirty my hands. "I don't feel like much, today."

The news was on, something about the price of crude, the threat of embargo. "Tommy says you work hard. How's seven an hour sound?"

"Fair. Real fair." It was more money than I'd ever made in my life, more than my old man had ever made.

He said, "Done," and told me to hand tape the corners, mud them in. "It don't have to be perfect," he threw in, the clack thud of his stilt feet sounding for all the world like poetry, like iamb, the old ham bone over the horseback, or that's what I was thinking, that's how I'd explain Jake, just then.

My head: seven dollars an hour times eight hours made fifty-six, which, multiplied by five days a week, came up to almost three hundred—nearly twelve hundred a month, thirteen thousand or so a year. Shit. High on the hog.

Corners are slow and tricky. You must roll out enough tape to cover top to bottom, hand fold the center crease along the length, and trowel joint compound as you go. Air pockets screw everything up. I worked my way through two corners while Jake stilted and thumped about his business. Once, when we were close, he said, "Looky here. Dance floor in the sky," and clacked his metal feet together. All my life, I'd heard that black folk could either sing or dance. Jake could do neither, but his rough pirouette scuffed sparks on the hard concrete, and he laughed out loud like that for a moment, stilting the crude waltz, moments of fire infecting me. It was a version of this earth to remember.

By lunchtime, I'd mudded my way to the corner near the sanctuary doors, could feel the heft in my heart of what was inside, the plates full of cash under black Jesus' thorny head, the ripped-out eyes.

"I'm goin home," Jake told me, his face hovering up by the ceiling's chalky glint. "You want a plate of food?"

I lied that I had brought a sack today. "But I appreciate you asking."

Man size again, Jake left me alone in the fellowship hall, suppers and poker some nights, he had said. I *was* hungry, as I ever had been, and thought about the totem poles, the masks on Jake's wall, the fennel-flavored sausage balls in the good spaghetti, my mama's burned-up wedding dress.

My uncle rented forty acres, on the back of which was a three-room shack without a bathroom or running water. They'd tried to paint it with mismatched colors donated by neighborhood churches so that the inside was a multitude of shades, delineations of white, tan, buff, bone. Two sleeping bags were stretched in the small room; beside each bed, a box of army pants, shirts that came near Jimmy and my sizes, a couple pairs of holey socks, and, for some crazy reason, a shoehorn for each of us. Taped to one wall was a paper sack with *we love you* Magic-Markered across it, written in the hand of my people. My sixth-grade year on the free-lunch plan that even poor people laughed at, two rolls if you like, and I pictured myself breaking necks, strangling with my own hands every snot nose that ever snickered, whispered, wrote my name on the shithouse wall. Don't talk about white trash inside of my ear-shot. My mother went to bed for three months that winter, and my old man didn't come home one night for two years. Without electricity or butane, Jimmy and I cooked on a backyard wood fire, him toasting white bread, *s–s–s–s–s– cinnamon t–t–t–toast,* and me learning pasta al dente, butter melt, ketchup sauce, ketchup sandwich, hilarious.

Inside, the sanctuary was all the same, sweet warm air, carved doors, the falling middle aisle toward the outstretched hands of the black messiah. Flowers. Cash. Plates filled and overrunning, more it seemed, much more. At the altar, I touched it, felt it in my hands, smelled it, held it to my lips, and prayed out loud, Oh God, may you be as black as a hole in the night, may you reach down and pluck my eyes from my head, rip me and make me right. Beside the full plates, a sheet of paper was curled at the edges. Centered, on top, written in a fine hand, the heading said HONOR SYSTEM. TAKE ONLY WHAT YOU NEED. SIGN HERE. This was communal money, a way of making good for each other, food in hungry mouths, the honor system, manna from heaven. What were they thinking?

I left Fayetteville and Arkansas behind me that day. I wish that I could say that I signed my name beneath the ones that had come before, joined the host of those that needed, whose names held the honor of worth. *Niggers did it,* my people said. I grew up in my father's house. I am not a bad man. I've never killed anyone. The classroom where I teach now is a place of light. "Letter from a Birmingham Jail" sometimes gets quoted by heart, wept through. I don't live in a world of guilt and sorrow. I'm not a liar. I'm right here, talking to you. I'm shooting you straight. You think you know me. Let me ask you, a good person, just like me, let me ask you this: What happens when our silence thunders, so that even when the truth is told, the lie still heaves our hearts, heaps our words, our blue-black days and nights, our dreams and the dreams of our children; our children's children's children pay and pay and pay, and is the debt ever paid? Say? Will our trees bear strange fruit, the bloody red sun shine on rivers I've seen bloat up over their banks, muddy water in woodline graves from Memphis to Mobile to this place? Will the castrated man wake in his deep, dark wood, draw the severed penis from his mouth, take a breath of sweet earth air, and scream *hallelujah* or *goddamn* or *fuck you* or *I love you* or anything and all manner of things be well? Is that what we think?

PARADISE

Three floors down, across our alleyway, their faces hover on the car-wash wall, where black Jesus is throned in feathery light and terrible Holy Ghost wheels a misshapen horse. From the mural, these newly dead neither smile nor frown. They concentrate— eyes fixed earthward. This is the May after my brother has been killed, and I imagine him as the winged figure, beating air. Across the bedroom, Louisa, my fiancée, sleeps. She's going on three months, is starting to show. This morning, her pregnancy strikes me as a door back into the world, a stout rope flung from the past to the future. We will spit in fat death's face.

"Jack?" She says my name, eyes open. For three days, Louisa has dreaded today's job interview. Since I returned from it all, we've run her credit cards crazy. Now, she digs her heels into the waking world. Outside, the Paradise Robowash has kicked into gear.

I shut the window. Limousines from the embassies across town snake up the alley to the sparkling mouth. They hum past the part of the mural where new Jerusalem spirals upward through seas that give up their dead. Mammoth beasts hurl fire at earth as washed cars glint out from the other side. Color sprawls over the wall. Each night, street artists paint the faces of dead gang children whose wounds are now healed. Beneath the heads are death dates, stretching back three years to when the mural started. This second, their oily sheen catches sun. Shades of blackness go gold.

"Louisa. Are you sick?" Nothing comes back.

The vacuum man has his way with the interior of a long, white limo. Behind, the black car's tinted windows reflect a breathtaking serpent, dragging skeins of shed skin. Out of this, the alarm seems accidental. Our clock radio is tuned to classical, Louisa's morning music. She turns, sees me at the window, and vomits into the bedpan. A burst of woodwind escalates. "You're up?"

"They've filled the sky with faces."

Louisa says, "I can see." She has her father's musculature, his long bones, is from a family that never dies. "Be sick for me this morning." Louisa throws our comforter back, finds a tissue in the cuff of her pajama sleeve. "I'm tired of it."

I rise to empty her pan, what I'm good at lately. She kisses my cheek, stands, wraps herself into a velour robe—deep purple. Her bedpan is cool to my fingers.

"I need coffee," Louisa says. "And don't let me see food."

While she showers, I slip across Twelfth to a package store where a machine brews alongside displays of birds and cheap whiskey. An N Street whore snaps shut a pocket mirror as I return. She asks for a drink, and, for a reason that escapes me, I give her a sip of mine. The woman's lips make a delicate heart on the styro cup. I tear this portion off, let the breeze take it to a gutter.

Louisa asks for help. Dripping, she takes her coffee and brushes fingertips over a rack of skirts, a slinky Elvira suit from last Halloween. "Something that breathes."

I pick. She says, "No." A siren seems frozen on the street below. Clean limousines are reporting for duty.

"This. Or this?"

I touch a favorite, the black knee-length that brings out the yellow in her eyes. The closet is dark on my side. "I can't picture you taking dictation."

Louisa sniffs the skirt, inspects stitches, says, "I'd rather eat glass."

While I iron, Louisa makes her face. The bathroom is a thing to reckon with—even with the ironing board open, there's room to waste. A jacuzzi is built into the oversized tub where we conceived. That was before, when we'd laze into evenings, not even bothering to lift the needle when it caught the scratch midway through Billie Holiday's "Strange Fruit." We'd run hot water to the rim, engage the pulse jets, and strip each other in steamy updrafts. Of those nights, I recall a word said underwater, a candle wick sizzling, the phrase "for the wind to suck" sung over and over as we touched one another in jasmined water.

When I finish, Louisa unfurls the dress neck to knee. "Yea or nay?"

The unplugged iron hisses. "Fine. I like it. Why do they keep painting dead people on a car-wash wall?"

Louisa says, "You fixate." She's in the bedroom jerking drawers. Bracelets clink on her wrists, but what I hear is on an Arkansas hill, deep with brown-eyed Susan, where the *click, click, click* marks increments as the pulleys lower a dazzling gray casket and a lone jet carves white into the cobalt sky.

"Heels or flats?" She dangles a pair from each hand.

"Flats."

Our front room overlooks a street corner where dealers gather; their fingers splay upward as they scream *number four, number four,* their code for crystal meth. A pigeon has lit on our bay ledge. Louisa gathers the papers she'll need, packs them in a black briefcase where we keep the cash we've scraped together. "I'll call later this afternoon when I know something," she says. "Be listening."

I offer to cook dinner, anything. "What sounds good?"

"Whatever." Louisa wipes a smudge off the door intercom. She straps her purse across her chest, and we lean into an awkward kiss. Across the hall, a dog yelps before a husky voice says, "Baby, baby." I'm told to keep my fingers crossed.

"Luck," I throw in, and she is gone. You kiss someone, and they are gone.

Things are going holy on me. A glass is suddenly a porthole to the spirit world, the digits of a new dime's mint date add to the hours in a day. Sixty-six days have passed since I scaled that Arkansas wrecking-yard fence, sweet-talked a black shepherd, and found Jimmy's car under a light pole. I was after hours. The Grand Prix had been sawed in half—it was something to see. The speedometer said seventy-five, the air was on high cool, the rearview was missing. By flashlight, I could see head blood pooled, baptismal still, in each floorboard hollow. A garnet senior ring that the EMTs hadn't stolen shined in the coppery mix where gasoline formed intricate rainbows. I slipped the ring on my wedding finger and, later, had a time getting it off. That night, after the viewing, Louisa called long distance from D.C. with tears in her voice. How could we deal with a baby, now?

In the kitchen, magneted to the refrigerator door, a note in Louisa's hand tells me that *time is no healer.* The maxim riddles me. I have not worked since returning to D.C. It's time. My job at New York, New York—a restaurant in Arlington—is being held. It is not yet nine when I try on a tuxedo shirt, start shining my black shoes.

Before my brother was killed, I waited the lunch crowd, rambunctious folk from upstairs desks who gestured with forked spinach and smoked while they ate. I imagine myself invisible, serving everything down to one for the road without having to write; my memory stuns a six-top. But when I try the number, our phone is out. The cord leads into a wall jack, hidden behind a stereo speaker where Louisa's long, thin hand is printed in the dust. She's disconnected us. I don't know why, but register the dark inside the tiny jack. It is the sort one might find inside a sewn-shut eye. I plug in, dial the operator. When he answers, I hang up.

Dressed, I brush my gone-long hair, remove a Metro pass from Louisa's top dresser drawer, and walk into the morning ruckus. Rearing to my right, head high on the Paradise wall, a severed tongue has *shame* purpled onto its tip. I give a dollar to a homeless man.

New York, New York is in one of the twin Gannett towers, where the news of the world funnels through *USA Today*. Beyond the horseshoe-shaped bar, seen through racks of martini glasses and brandy snifters, the neon jukebox sings Sinatra's version of "New York, New York." This theme song is played, I recall, every nineteen minutes on the dot. Nineteen, my brother at age of death, on the ninth, the wreck occurring on State Road 319. My arrival is unexpected; two waitresses whisper to each other over the ice bin. Bearden—the day manager, whose job it had been to tell me— ushers us into a clean, windowless office. His desktop is perfect, not even a stray paper clip or thumbprint on the glass.

"What's happened to you, Jack?" A vein quickens near the corner of a deep-blue eye. "Why didn't you stay in touch?"

I say, "I've lost time." It occurs to me that I should have gotten my hair cut before this meeting. "And I'm going to be a father. I've known for a while."

Bearden removes a handkerchief from his breast pocket, wipes an invisible mark from the glass-covered desk. He says, "Congratulations, son. You lose someone, you find someone."

"What?"

"Lose somebody, find somebody."

"That makes sense. Sure."

Bearden triple folds the handkerchief, replaces it in his pocket. "It's been two months. You should have called," he says. "If you still want to work here. Do you still expect to work here? For New York, New York?"

I picture Louisa charming her way though the otherworldly questions that get asked during interviews—What is the most horrible thing you've ever done that you're not ashamed of? Do you still tell lies? "I'd like to. Yes sir." I shift my face to where he's looking.

"Are you *over* your brother?"

I say, "Yessir," what he needs to hear.

"You sure? Positive?"

"Yeah."

"Good," he says. "Don't dwell." A hair net gets offered across the desk's mirrored surface. "You can expedite with Cholley. He's the day sous-chef, now."

"I appreciate it," I say, and stand.

"Watch your ass," he tells me, and we shake. Before I'm dismissed, he asks, "You want a boy or girl?"

I say, "Doesn't matter," and walk out.

Behind the expediter station, Cholley sharpens a chef's knife on long steel. Without missing a beat, he sails a time card my way and insists that I start on condiments—the job no one wants.

I begin with ketchup. The trick is to arrange the fifty unfilled bottles around a lazy Susan. The night people have shined each clean so that the caps show only pink residue. Next, the plastic bladder of wholesale—passed off as Heinz—must be retrieved from cold storage, a dark room where I used to steal a strawberry, a raw oyster. With kitchen shears, you must snip the bag's underside spout, then sway it, slowly, to the first bottle's mouth. Pass the bladder over each bottle, eight, nine seconds, long enough to fill three-quarters. As I sidestep to the third bottle, snippets of my past life fire away at me: Louisa's lips are printed on a love letter I've shredded, feisty organ music cascades from thrown-open sanctuary doors, Jimmy walks out into Sunday morning glare, six feet tall, sawdust bronze, song on his lips. I miscalculate on bottle eight, spill onto nine, which in turn ruins ten, eleven, and twelve. Once you mess this job up, there's no making it stop. Cholley snorts; an entire countertop is being spoiled.

Trying to right my wrong, I knock bottle thirteen hard into fourteen. The two strike each other lip to lip. Glass breaks, not a lot, but enough. The fat ketchup sack leaks onto the white floor. Cholley lays down his blade; both of us know the rule on infection. I must wash out the whole lot, each of the fifty bottles, or open New York, New York to the risk of sliced tongues, gut slivers, whopping lawsuits. I hoist the sack, though, start filling number fifteen.

Before I can finish, Cholley has marched Bearden into the

kitchen. The manager stands beside a glass box, set on wheels; inside, seared baby-back ribs, a split roasted chicken, are artfully arranged—ready for display. Bearden says, "You're not well, Jack. You shouldn't have come here. You should have stayed in touch." He retrieves an apron from under the rib display, ties it over a crisp, white shirt. The dripping bag is taken from my hands. Bearden says, "Clock out."

Louisa has encouraged me to open up, to say what I'm thinking. "I'm sorry," I say, "I don't want to clock out. I'm fine," but the two men ignore me. They set to repairing my damage.

I wash up in the men's room, which is all big mirrors and hidden lights, so everywhere is my shining, ketchup-spattered self staring back. This is where Bearden told me about the car wreck, his left hand on my right shoulder. A few seconds passed that way. It was odd, I had thought then, for the manager to lay his hand on me in the men's room. My brother was dead. He'd crashed his truck. I was to take care of business. Get over it. Stay in touch.

Now, as I walk out through the foyer, the hostess who calls herself Persian looks down at the carpet. Behind my back, Sinatra lists into a spirited climax—*if you can make it here, you can make it anywhere.* I step onto the down escalator and am whisked toward a day that is undoing itself. I can't help remembering the *other* day, how everything had seemed so newly deformed.

Riders on the Metro act as though they've never seen anything like me before. They let me take any seat I desire, abandon fresh copies of the *Post, USA Today.* Even two young gangsters steer clear. I say, "It's not bad," and dab a fingertip from my messed-up shirt, taste it. They half smile. We begin to move, soon pass below the Potomac River, where moist rivulets mark pressure points in the deep tunnel. My ears pop. This part of my once-daily commute has always baffled me; how does one explain being a passenger in a craft that passes below a riverbed? How can such a thing be thought? Before, I'd try to hold a breath from one side to the other. I'd imagine the red-lit walls crushing in on my last words, see my grieving people—Louisa in the lead—kiss my cold forehead one last time, slip their holiest good-byes into the heart side of my coat, request hair clippings. But today it's just a tunnel, a built thing, a way to get from one place to the other.

"Tell me what's wrong with you, son?" Behind me, a tourist couple carry bags from the National Gallery. The woman's eyes are watery green. Her T-shirt says, DON'T BLAME ME.

"Me?"

She says, "Who else?" The man with her wears a wrist brace. On one finger, a diamond is embedded in raised gold. He covers the ring with his good hand, shakes his head side to side.

"Nothing's wrong with me," I say.

We've reached the point where the tracks begin to rise; above us, jets trace this stretch of river toward International. "On our piece of earth," the woman says, shaking a crooked finger in her husband's face, "we still reckernize a fellow in trouble." Her purse snaps open and a crisp five-dollar bill gets handed over the seat, catching the eyes of the two young hoodlums. They stare, sway with each jolt.

I accept, for some reason say, "Bless you."

"Sugar? We got a friend who bled for us. Don't you ferget that." She shuts her purse, touches the husband's stricken hand.

On the escalator up, I fold the paper money until all that shows are three black serial numbers—*seven, seven, seven*. Alone, I am taken up toward the world of light, just now blue as my brother's eyes. *Luck, luck, luck,* I think, *Louisa.* My heart beats hard. I can't say why, but I start to jog up the metal steps. Soon, I'm three at a time, calves knotting. The end is a dead sprint. Up through the portal gate, I'm delivered into air that shines sweet enough to slice.

Across Twelfth, the Paradise has emptied. A vacuum man rolls hose into coils, while another push brooms the alley. Small piles of loose asphalt gather every few feet in front of the mural's lower world. Here the faces multiply, aswirl in color, forty yards of chaos rising toward the black savior. It comes over me to kneel at the halved Red Sea, below the feet of African Moses. His one volcanic eye blasts over Pharaoh's crippled chariot and me as slave children scream *hallelujah*. Good Samaritan's gaunt cheeks have thinned to bare concrete. Prissy Satan seems bored.

Inside, Louisa isn't home. I strip and shower, dress in clean clothes. Louisa keeps cabernet in the cabinet. A little is good for the stomach, for the heart. I pour out a glass for each of us, inspect the telephone again, and tune the stereo to a full-gospel station—the music of my childhood. Though I no longer believe, the Baptist in me still relishes a stiff drink had to the hand-clapped rhythm of Holy Rollers. Louisa is lapsed Episcopalian, watered-down hymns and afternoon teas. I toast her glass, swallow. By now, "New York, New York" has arrived at its seventh singing. Our apartment is filled with tambourine and fiddle—voices like rain on tin.

The trick to marinara is two garlic heads, broad sided, fine diced, glazed in extra-virgin oil. I let three fat bulbs have it, throw a handful into the skillet, and the air goes festive—rich. I imagine Louisa here, a baby boy sleeping on our bed, us toasting a future where trouble is as alien as words spoken underwater. A quartet jumps into a fiery rendition of "Pow'r in the Blood," and I tap my toes as a number ten can of tomatoes gets emptied. The mashed fruits sizzle. Next, I pry open an anchovy tin, take a whiff, then bite into a tiny fillet, a lacy skeleton. They go in, oil and all. I let fly two heavy sloshes of wine, go to town on a bunch of parsley. Louisa has complained that our kitchen has no light, no windows. "Why not just cook naked?" she once asked, then proceeded to make Belgian waffles in nothing but a shorty red apron. I hear "wonder working power" and think *Louisa* as the day rolls on outside where horror and joy, brute and healer, really *do* lay together in wait, hands clasped for the ambush.

Our oven clock says a little after two. The airwaves have lulled. I know without looking that there's not a cloud in the sky. To my left, through the kitchen's arched passway, our heavy front door, and beyond that, down three flights and two doors, is N Street, which leads out past the Paradise to DuPont, to the Beltway, on out through Maryland to the barrier islands, to the blue-cold Atlantic, where weary ships full of seagoers named the land for what they'd left behind. This is a moment when I believe in the great, wide-open spaces, see promise beyond the confines of rooms without windows. I take a drink from my partner's glass and almost pray out loud.

Before it even hits me that she's home, Louisa is through the front door, down the hall. Her keys dangle from the bolt lock. Behind our bedroom's slammed-shut door, mattress springs twang. Her flats thud to the floor. On the radio, the news is about what's happening overseas, more about a peace plan gone sour, the imminence of retaliation.

Inside our room, what I can see of her face is flushed, buried into a pillow. I say, "Louisa?" and kneel beside the bed, beside the bedpan, which is really just a paint roller pan. Through the window, the sun is at an angle that makes the room seem like Sunday afternoon—sad, just waiting for the new day. "What's wrong?"

Her shoulder is hard beneath my hand. A hefty lump bulges like a child's diaper under the black skirt. I smell something sweet-flowery-familiar but can't put my finger on why it rings a bell. I touch the back of Louisa's head.

"Leave me alone." She says the words one hard syllable at a time.

I say, "It's okay," and brush a piece of white lint from the fine hairs on the side of her face. What I want is to arrest time, to go back. "Tell me. What happened?"

Louisa says, "The baby's gone. I want to be alone."

"Gone? What do you mean, gone?"

"I called. Why wouldn't you answer?"

I ask her to look at me, but she won't. "Are you okay. Are you hurt?"

"I miscarried." Louisa makes a sound that is something between a laugh and a sob—I can't tell. She keeps her face from mine. She says, "The stove . . . something's burning."

"Why won't you look at me?" Questions I don't have words for shotgun though my head; one numb knee cracks. "Louisa?"

"What?"

I touch the thin dress fabric, her back, her stomach. In the front room, where my music is all wrong, the phone rings. "Tell me what's happened."

"You," she says. Through teeth, "You."

We fight. Lines are drawn, crossed. At first, she denies, tells me that I'm the cruelest man on earth to accuse her of such a thing after what she's been through. She claims that she *tried* to reach me, that the doctors let the phone ring off the wall, that neighbors pounded our front door. Maybe the phone rang and I didn't hear it. But then I remember the disconnected cord, her handprint, and *know* and *know* and *know* why. Things get thrown out the window, out of our lives. I pack everything I own, tell her to have a good goddamn life. My marinara sauce stains the ceiling, and a photograph of my brother, Jimmy, is ripped to pieces, pieces into pieces. Finally she admits what we've known for months, and it comes as sudden as the ashtray that burst our dining-room display of family photographs. Louisa shocks me back into the world. She says that she does not intend to go on paying for a loss that was beyond her. My brother was nobody to her; she'd never even met him. And under no circumstances would she ever bear a child meant to take his place, to lift him out of the grave. I do not expect to hear such a thing said outright, and the force of what has happened—of our lost child—shames me to the core. The truth of this last thing, how it tears me, will haunt us, but all that's around the bend, invisible as unbreathed air.

Later, I leave our bedroom door an inch or two ajar and stand there listening long enough to hear Louisa get out of bed and begin to undress. I strain to hear these small movements.

I remove Louisa's keys from the front door. The stairs creak as I make my way down.

Outside, in the alley between us and the Paradise, three neighbor kids play stickball with a dented beer can. A tall one has a turn at hitting, and another stands deep to catch the can as it ricochets off the mural wall. They go on, as if I'm not there. The boy who pitches is ten, twelve, maybe. His windup is exaggerated—a thing to see—and the can whizzes off his fingertips before the other swings a makeshift bat, misses a few times before connecting. They talk trash, kick imaginary rivals with untied shoes, the tongues of which flap wildly. They call the faces in the blue mural by name. When the hitter fakes a bunt, the one in the field, a boy who says little but whose eyes are intent as a judge's, is not fooled. His feet are planted; he waits for what will come.

I watch them this way for a while and am almost tempted to join. This is the sort of ramshackle fun that, late of an afternoon, would make Louisa giddy—and she'd play with all her heart. Please, please look down on all this, get up and look through the window, see what a spectacle.

Just before dark, the boys rally for one last play. The pitcher goes into an elaborate windup, seems about to fall before the can spins forward, flips head over tail. The batter's chest-high swing is true, lightning through still air. As he follows through, the smashed can arcs high, sings up as though winged and hell-bent on escape. I hear a hammer wallop, a sound that seems to both begin and end. The sure, sullen fielder lifts his gold eyes, sees the can spin hard up over the topmost wispy clouds of the kingdom, escaping even the outstretched hand of an angry God, moving out toward whatever has grown dark on the other side. We freeze beneath this brief magic. Above us, brushed onto the pale sky, are the faces of those who have gone before and now blaze in the tongued fire of today's last light. Our collective shriek severs the vision. *Paradise?* This is what I've seen.

They sing, "Jesus," and "Christ," and leap into each other's arms as if gods and heraldic beasts had stepped down to live among us.

CRYSTAL CITY

Louisa kept telling me I had to go home. "Face it," she'd say, late of an afternoon, when my session was over and we were just people again, walking home from the Metro to the row house we shared. She'd finished college, was a counselor for the city, close pored and sudden with a tender spot for fuckups like me. She owned a pickup, a red GMC for what it's worth, and was hell-bent on driving me home since I'd never go in a million years. We'd known each other for a while—she had papers on me.

I paid gas. On the summer solstice, we hit the road, from D.C. down through Knoxville to Memphis, where the river bridge bleeds on in to Arkansas and that long stretch of plowed earth between places. Down home, Louisa and me, *facing it*.

Louisa'd never gone south. "I want to live here," she said. "Right out in yonder field. Look."

Outside Forrest City, crop-duster jalopies dive-bombed the highway, gauzy sprays tight on the land where my people lay buried. A buckled farmhouse shone under ripped tin, knee-high milo up to the front step.

"Yonder?"

"You say that. 'Yonder this. Yonder that.'"

The pilots were genuine whackos. They'd buzz you in a second, waggle out old cholly, and piss down on you from their seats. Best not to look them in the eye, too many fumes. Construction barrels lined the fast lane, fecund bayou water up to the curb gutter where frog gigging was out of this world about this time of year.

"It's what we call heaven. 'Over yonder.' You never heard me talk about heaven."

Louisa said, "Honey. That's all you ever talk about."

One silver duster zinged out in front of us, the loud snicker sickening my stomach. Louisa waved, honked.

"Don't provoke the son of a bitch."

"Your mother. Her boyfriend—what's his name. Jimmy. Your grandfather Si. All *over yonder*."

"You talking about my mama?"

"That, too. All that mama baggage."

Skimming the orange barrels, the duster glided into a stall. The pilot—a girl with a shock of red hair snapping—mouthed something, hurled a fistful of weeds or flowers or a beer can, I couldn't tell, then humped ass skyward.

"Paradise," Louisa said. "How can you not be positively freaking in love with this?"

Her rear struts were history—a spring was gone, and the other was going. She burned oil—a quart a tank. The column shifter ground. Her wipers were useless. We'd had a bucked-up ride from the Beltway on. "Give it time," I said. "I bet this old Jimmy makes it."

The transmission went just south of Hot Springs—first, second, third, all but reverse. So we eased our way on toward Crystal City, crawdad backwards, passersby making that fish-eye look like we'd grown pitchforks or dildos out of our heads. Around us, the Ouachita Mountains—worn down volcanoes, rockhound shops where slag glass graced tables aside hunks of quartz crystal—lucent as eyelens. Past the *Last* Chance and the *Last Last* Chance liquor stores, Joplin Worm & Video, Crystal City Jail,

Louisa held the line. Summer solstice, a rain had fallen, steam sliding off into the woods.

A far-off piece of lake came through the trees, blue and real.

"Look at us, bass-akwards." She twisted and smiled, gunned the broken-down truck back over a one-lane bridge. "What we have here's again the law. Say Jacky? We gonna be arrested?"

Folk were getting baptized off boathouse row, a lank, black-haired man taking them down by the neck and shoulders. Out under the good sun, the last of the rented ski boats circled home, a few rainbow sails rivaling the blue sky. A dozen, they were out in the shallows, away from the slotted boat ramp where one-legged Grandpa Si taught me to swim. Bass hit after mud minnows—made circles, those circles, circles. A pair of shiny black Labs swam among the Christians, boat paddles crossways in their mouths. Their wakes rippled through the white-sheeted seven or eight who sang *hallelujahs*. The preacher's jubilations were spicy, joy infected; against hellfire's damnation, he screamed *luh-ove lift-it me,* words in my mother's tongue.

Waist-deep down the boat ramp, water clear enough to see our feet, Louisa and I watched and sipped gins. We'd steered clear of saying anything tough. I told her about Zydeco, Si's three-legged Shih Tzu, about the day we went blackberrying on Mount Nebo, where copperheads sunned in rock piles sweet with sticker vines.

Now, sun cut shaft-prisms down through the water.

Louisa was silent, nodded, seemed transfixed by the baptisms. She'd been raised Episcopalian, *whiskopalian,* she'd say.

Two of the flock women sang out *shall we gather,* sweet voices that made me want to cry—crazy.

Si was an amputee, had lost one leg while chainsawing firewood, an accident that sent my young mama riding in the ambulance, loosening and tightening the tourniquet all the way from Danville Mountain to Russellville. The sawed-off leg in her lap, and the hospital lawn filled with friends on blankets, scores, because Si was a minor-league ballplayer then for the Dixie League—but all that, how he'd get phantom charley horses in the missing limb and got hooked on morphine and had to fly off to

New York City to get off, all that's another story, one my mother tried to keep from me. Anyway, one snake—a gleaming two-footer—struck the flesh-colored calf on Si's bare prosthesis, where a purple heart was lightning zigzagged. Si'd stomp, and the snake would strike. The copperhead would strike, and Si'd stomp. Venom leaked down into his shoe foot.

"Shake a leg," I said. "Everone's heard that story."

Taller Louisa, her neck skin showed chill bumps down to the halter V. "Your mother, the tourniquet part. Are you making that up. Is that a lie? Because that's the story. That's what this is all about. I think so, anyway. Jesus, imagine."

"It's close to true."

Louisa said, "One way or the other."

Now, kids on the boat dock fed out corn kernels to lunkers, bass named *Big Arkie* or *Bucket Mouth* or *Beelzebub* that I'd probably sometime fed myself. Once, I watched a full-grown mallard dragged down to where fish slabs from the cleaning station glowed pale as hands.

"Something's biting my foot."

A yellow-haired girl come up fighting tears or laughter. In paper cups, our blue gins ticked.

"Something keeps biting my foot. What's down there?"

"Water moccasins, liable to be. They mate on boat ramps."

Water, a cold handful, slapped my face. Louisa made two fingers into fangs, struck my throat. "Now or never," she said, her brown eyes the color of plowed dirt on a morning after the first frost when the smell of leaf fire comes.

One of the reborn looked our way, then she went on getting reborn, which was fine by me because I'd been that once.

"Bluegill. They'll eat your moles."

The preacher petted one of the swimming dogs, then lifted his face, sang out vowels that carried over water. They weren't so bad, really, the Jesus people.

"Oh, hell, what do you need me for?" Louisa sank her cup, leaned out into the water, and floated on her back. "I'm peeing," she said. "I'm swimming and peeing. Bluegill fish eating my moles. Swimming and peeing."

Away from me, swimming and peeing.

Earlier, old Og hadn't known me from Adam, but when I said *Si,* he smiled and said *no shit.* He recalled snippets of my story from the newspapers. His big dirt-colored hands still palsied. Og had a man who knew the inside of a clutch by heart. He'd get on it right now. I was offered a room down by the water with a toilet, kitchenette, and a queen-sized bed with a mattress that hadn't been pissed on yet.

"Your mama, son," he said. "And that fellow? What year was that? I can't remember shit."

In his office, ten-pound bass were mounted on each of the four walls. A window-unit cooler blew papers off his desk, ruffling the Polaroids tacked up on corkboard. Up there somewhere, Si.

"Seventy-three."

"I'll be damned. No shit." The old dark man looked down on me through milky cataracts. "And what year's this?" He said, "Looky here." Inside the empty ice bucket was a silver key on a ten-inch hookless Rapala lure and a wrinkled picture.

Outside, in the daylight, my grandfather's face grew rowdy. Under the gold lure, Si shined.

Louisa swam away, toward the deep water where a red-white-and-blue buoy marked the no-wake line. One Lab saw her and paddled that way for a while, then stopped.

Out in the channel, a motor died.

Who knew?

Twenty-five years ago, when my mother and her boyfriend Frank Bottoms were at each other's throats, Si would show up with a sack full of tomatoes, a salty joke, saying he'd *open up a can of whipass* on all of us, especially Frank. He'd smell like Ancient Age and Catfish Charley and himself. These appearances coincided with bad fight days. And there'd be Si, my mama's old man, banging the screen door with a skinned-up fist, full of piss and strong magic. He'd trade tomatoes for my clothes, eye the two of them until everyone got quiet and nervous, then dare them with an insult-rife story, and laugh until the table light shook. When we'd drive off toward Crystal City, behind us, back in the hot rent house, dust would settle. For a while, my people'd stop trying to kill each other dead.

Louisa lapped the buoy in long, strong strokes as the newly

baptized filed past me, up the concrete boat ramp toward Shangri-la. The wet, happy dogs scouted out in front of them, retrieved boat paddles sculling out from their jaws.

In the east, already, pale Vega, the summer triangle.

"It's beautiful," Louisa said, out of breath. "I believe you." She swung her hair one way and the other, breathing out lemon in my face. "You've way underplayed this place."

A way off beyond the dam bridge, on the riverside, wood smoke rose up from an invisible hollow. Someone was always down there drinking Black Label, dumping illegal kills, burying carcass, up to no good.

I said, "That's not true."

Fish gills. Fish for me. Something's fishy. Will you think, please, of fish. Fresh fish. Fish on Friday. Teach a kid to fish. Flying fish. Slippery fish. Other fish to fry. Fishing expedition. Fish eye. Dead fish. Fish and loaves. Fish belly. Fish spawn. Swims like a fish. Fish— the shining noun that verbs itself. Jesus ate fish, Buddha—fish, Lao Tzu, Gollum, Caesar, my mama, me, tell me a fish story, salmon, pompano, smallmouth, walleye, holy rainbow trout. Fillet steaks cut off blue channel cats that swam today, that sweet-water smell still on them. Bass, crappie, channel cat, bluegill, let them soak an hour in stale beer, egg, stout yellow mustard, cayenne pepper. Pour yellow cornmeal, good tempura flour, Zatarain's is best, in a steel bowl and have lard oil hot in cast iron, medium-high flame. Oh Jesus, cook with gas every chance you get and shake your soaked fillets in Zatarain's, fry them gold, take time because it's a good day when you're not in the grave and can cook fish that swam today in water once come down from crashed comets. Pour the flour with yellow cornmeal and lay in chopped spring onion, your stale beer and egg. Ball this into hush puppies, spoon them in til they hiss in the fish oil and go gold, lay them leak beside the gone-firm fillets. Carve, squeeze lemon halves (big Myers from Rancho Pedro's in Melbourne Beach, Florida, if you can get them) on your fish while new-potato wedges make cicada ruckus in the powerful air. Cook, son, daughter, brother, sister, fa-

ther, mother know temperature by sound. Slice homegrown tomatoes, double-fister Big Boys, grown scarlet under August, cut
finger thick and coarse salted beside purple onion, sweet banana
pepper, jalapeño, cayenne, bread and butter pickles, coleslaw
made with mayonnaise sprinkled with fresh-cut dill, set beside
bowls full of ham-spiked purple hulls, tartar and cocktail sauce.
Call the carrier of the big bottled beers, iced for three days
straight in a horse trough where ruby-red Congo melons sweat.
Eat outside by the dock on the lake where tourists dry their wet
money and mosquitoes dodge fast bats under ecliptic shade.
Think about how it might be to go home to Arkansas, where
people eat such. Consider the moment when you understand that
nobody's coming at you from behind your back. You're okay, you
made it, you're eating fish. Fill a plate in summer with a lover, under the Ouachita moon, in a place that was once a refuge, a place
you've been during deep trouble.

Fish for me.

After supper, in dark number seven, Louisa bathed, the mellow
hiss of water's gurgle. On humid air, her scrubbed skin. I was not
alone, which means something when you've been that way.
Through the open door, lights beginning at the boatel stretched
en regatta clear to Crystal City, where you couldn't tell volcanic
mountain from sky, deep fields, diamonds.

"I still feel like I'm in that truck."

The bed was too soft. I lay on the floor beside it, listened.

"Your truck's over yonder. We're here."

The water was close, I could hear it on the banks where some
boys night-fished the tip of the cove. Their lead *kerplunked*, and
the night went noisy with bullfrog. June bugs thumped into the
walls. One of their reels, the boys down on the bank, had grit in
the gearbox, you could hear the grind.

"This room. It's nice of that guy. Og. I like it."

Someone below us farted, and the others cracked up. I smelled
cigarette smoke. They were having a time. The rowdy dogs were
back, shadows sculling amongst the boys.

"I never stayed here."

"Who gets named Og?"

My back felt better, on the cool floor. The boys out on the bank, I wanted to tell them that they'd be okay. That whatever they came up against could be gotten around. Their friends, their brothers may die, they'd hang tight.

I said, "It's *go*, backwards."

"Make me laugh. Ha." Invisible, Louisa's feet swished the floor. She couldn't see me, and I couldn't see her. But we knew that we were there. Like after Si barged into the kitchen on my parents, saying *I'm ding dong daddy from Dumas* or some silly shit.

When she stepped on me, my back cracked.

"Jesus. *God,*" Louisa said, and tumbled onto the mattress, the springs of which let loose a squall. And she was laughing.

Down on the water, a voice said, "*Je-sus. God. Je-sus. God.*"

"Where *are* you?"

"Down here."

"Well get your ass up here. I just stepped on you."

"I'll show you Si's. Tomorrow."

"Now. Up here, now. I'm adding all this up. In my head."

Out under the gaudy stars that I'd learned at the feet of a man with one foot, one of them was singing. It was the dumb-ass hundred-bottles-of-beer song that I'd forgotten ever hearing. The high voice cracked and deepened. Another wolf howled, and a cigarette spanked and waggled. Flat shale rock skipped eleven, twelve, thirteen times across the silver water. Seeing Si's face, things *could* go holy on you.

"Now? Now's not now anymore," I said.

"Hillbilly existentialist. Cut the shit."

"In a minute."

"Now."

Places in between?

Si'd lost his leg in the Solgahatchia bottom, near Lanty and Morrilton, where the Treadwells owned land on the Trail of Tears. His prosthesis, framed in a silver brace, was tattooed all up and down with the loopy signatures of the fishing parties he'd guided

on Ouachita. Here were colorful naked ladies named Colleen and
Lilah and Velva, heraldic beasts and Old Testament fire, a great
wicked world coalescing in what, to thirteen-year-old me, seemed
infinitely more real than flesh.

"The fakirs," he said on an August evening, 1973, red-hearted
Scorpius marking the way to what Si claimed was the galaxy's
soul, "a-spin themselves in circles and hang upside down. We
don't have to do that."

"Spin circles?"

"Or starve. We won't have to starve ourselves either."

That night we'd gorged on green-tomato pie, shortbread, and
buttermilk. I said, "That's good, not starving."

Three miles from Shangri-la boat dock, down gravel that turned
to dirt, past the hog killer and Stagger's corn plot, his tin trailer
seesawed a little. The garden was a rock's throw west. We sat between the tomatoes, okra, and bloom-flowery butternut. It was
still hot. We'd stripped off for forays through the hose sprinkler,
Si—liquored up on his wood leg—and me, the me I used to be.

"Ain't necessary to hang upside down."

"I'm glad."

"Look at me. Here. You don't got to be no genius to commune
with you future self."

Sometimes, happy with sweet bourbon, he'd damn Frank Bottoms to hell, doctor his sentences with hammered fists and
snapped teeth. Red-faced warlock, he'd cuss blistering mouthfuls
at Mama's lover, who'd been hitting her lately with a closed fist,
blacking her eyes so she'd have to say she'd walked into a door or
fallen out of bed. He'd throw his face back, scream, "Oh God.
Damn. Don't. Let. The son of a bitch. Die. Before I kill him," and
I'd feel infected as a smoker's lung long after he passed out.

"I like that," I said. "Commune with my future self."

Si said, "Simple," stood on one foot, danced a loose jig through
the hose sprinkler's rainbow.

We were naked. Happy hour had stretched long after supper. I
was aware of my penis, covered it with one hand, dirt going where
dirt goes. During our passings through the cold well water, my
grandfather's pecker bounced this way and that, crooked and
ruddy against his thigh; strange things, dicks.

This was the summer when *it* was going to happen, when the thing between my mother and Frank was an icy comet come rocketing toward us. Shit would hit the fan soon. But I didn't see that then, not one inkling. Maybe Si saw some and fortified himself thusly. I don't know.

"See here."

Si went to one knee, fanned dirt, then picked out a piece of quartz crystal, the lump size of a testicle or a baby's fist.

"What's at sposed to do?"

He tossed it—through the air between us. "A goddamn rock. Or a crystal ball. Same thing. Look through it."

I obeyed. At arm's length, the quartz was hard and cool and new against my right eye. "I don't see a thing. Dark light."

His knee stump was blistered above the leg's hellfire, and I thought of my mama turning the tourniquet. "Yeah. What else?"

It was honestly neither light nor dark. My hair was wet, I could feel it drip down my neck. "You. Not good." I cupped my hand around the rock so light came through. "I can see your leg. A little. I can tell you're there."

"That's right. That one thing."

"What?"

In my hand, for any fool to see, the crystal dopplered, red shifted and blue shifted; red meant the source body rushed away, blue signaled approach at light speed. What Simon said was bone simple: lift eyes on any clear night, and starlight will rush you back through time. Say *fossil light,* hold that hard *f* and *t* against your teeth—your soul, a mouthful, no? We are carbon; carbon forms from exploded stars—sixth-grade stuff. And believe you me, I sensed in that hole between us something that shouldn't be forgotten, a gust of buried fish gut rotting into the winter collards.

"Get my trousers, Jackey-boy. I'm Humphrey the Camel."

Si snickered. Lightning bugs stung all around us. I passed him the rock. He put my crystal back in the dirt, beat it down with a backhand, stood, and stomped.

A chill came. I was flesh and blood.

What I remember of the spring: crocus to yellow forsythia, my mother's jonquils, dogwood, and the sulfur smell of tornado warnings howling off in Bayou Meta. In a photo before the fire, her brown eyes tilt up toward the camera, verge on some hilarity that breaks her face into smile and then laughter and what always comes after. Once, at night, she sang out my name, said to get help. *He* was killing her, she hollered. Afraid, I covered tight. Certain things I've thought through: the percussive wallop a fist makes through sheetrock, a wall stud breaking, the way burnt hair smells. We are Southern people. Put us in a roomful of strangers, and we'll hold our tongues, cook a fish supper, pour out our last drink, give you our bed, our last four dollars. Shut us behind any hollow-core door, and, if we're of the mood, if we've had enough, we'll kick your ass into next week. And if we *love* someone, deeply *love* someone, why we're liable to kick their by-god ass to kingdom come. We'll cross the line. They were like that, my mother and Frank, crosscurrents, bad dreams electric in their blood. *Deep* in love.

I tried for a time to go to sleep, to turn loose. But the noisy boys were wired. They'd sung their way down from a hundred to zero and were at it all over again, *take one down, pass it around.*

Come sunshine, Louisa and I walked the three miles to Si's. Sunday morning, deep shades winding across the wide, quiet water— walls of time waving. The Holy Rollers were finishing a sunrise service on boathouse row. Their clothes were colorful. You could hear them singing Dixieland sweet, the words ringing. I wished that I was a Christian again and knew that I'd never would be; my life had turned another way.

We took cups of hot coffee from a bright-eyed waitress at Shangri-la and walked up the hill, past the motor shed, where a foot stuck out from under Louisa's truck, heel clacking, keeping time.

Best not to talk. Be reverent on the dirt road that takes you back. 1973. When it happened.

Louisa walked up in front of me. She didn't know where she was going, what she was in for; neither did I.

Down the potholed road, old Staggers's place, the hog butcher's field, the tree with the Ancient Age whiskey bottle grown

into its fork, all of it was plain, plain. The road forked by the rot-
ted mailbox post. Gravel went to dirt and dirt to dust. Twenty-five
years ago, I wouldn't have known that I'd ever meet Louisa or
even make it past thirteen. Simple as white bread, I wouldn't have
pictured me or my people buried on a hill that overlooked a light-
ning-struck tree where cows chewed grass.

We were close.

The clearing was grown up, but the trailer was still there, forever unmoored, bucking up a little with Zydeco's silly doggy door
come off its hinges. Growth blotted out the rock wall, the boat-
motor stump, and the compost heap. Trees had taken the sky.

Louisa said, "Here?"

The screened-in porch was missing screens, and the ancient
chest freezer was padlocked shut. I had no urge to go inside. Outside, under the sky, that was best. 1973, our last summer, before Si
took me home, where we found my mother, was hellacious hot.
We slept outside on grassy pallets, sang gospel songs. I first tasted
hard liquor on a night with wood smoke rising while we gave
chorus to "Pow'r in the Blood."

"Here. But it's changed. It didn't look like this."

"Guide me through. How different?" Wedged into the worm-
wood door, Louisa found a piece of metal with *Treadwell* stamped
into it. It was my mother's maiden name, odd for a one-legged
man. "How was it different?"

I wanted no part of what was dark inside under the ramshackle roof, beyond the cracked, Scotch-taped windowpane. It
had all been gone through, anyway. "I don't know. I can't say."

Louisa pulled the porch swing six inches toward her, let it fall.
The thing swung back, then forward, made a sound like casket
pulleys—a sound once heard, never forgotten. She said, "Your
porch of spirits lingering?"

"Somebody needs to tear it the fuck down."

We walked west, toward the spot. We wouldn't find it, that was
fine. It didn't matter. The garden had gone.

I said, "This's close," and we rested, sun-warmed hoppers whir-
ring.

Louisa took her sandals off, combed a woolly weed between
her legs, bent it between her fingers, then moved to another. She

was smart, had been to college. All her people were university people. They hung tight together, had poolside vodka tonics on Sundays—never killed each other. Louisa, she had an open heart. She believed that people were okay, could love each other and get on, and that's a belief I've always wanted for myself.

"Get your story straight," she said. "Shoot." She drew a line between us with her finger. She'd wait all day.

I said, "We got caught of course."

What I needed was a drink of sweet water. Strung up on a piece of cord from the chinaberry tree, a hummingbird feeder gourd swayed and went still. I, myself, had filled it forever with red sugar water from a ladder I'd no longer need.

"No one was there. When Si took me home. To my house. Where we lived then, outside Lonoke."

"Okay."

"Where those silos were. That crop duster."

Louisa wasn't afraid of me, or at least she didn't show. That touched me. Walk down the street, see me, and look down, that's how it's always seemed to me with people.

"The flying girl. Right."

"Mama's clothes were piled up out on the patio. Her whole half of the closet and shoes and hair barrettes. Her toothbrush. A couple hats and a wig, and some of my stuff, too, it'd all been put on fire. A gas fire. She, Mama, wasn't there. No one was home. Someone'd left the milk out, and ants had got into it. Si said for me to stay where I was. While he looked around."

Louisa's face was unearthly peaceful, clear as Jesus. A vehicle was coming up the way we'd walked, moving slow our way.

"So Si went looking. For Mama and Frank-daddy. I got the broom and swept. But I couldn't figure out about the clothes. Shirts and pants, bras. Her wedding dress. What do you make of a burnt-up wedding dress?"

Louisa fingered a piece of rock, ran it along the veins on her backhand. She had this way of nodding while you talked, some people can do that. Up on the road, gears downshifted.

"I found her behind the yellow forsythia bush. Out front where the water hose was. She'd been put out. I could tell it was her right off. Her eyes were open, she was breathing funny."

A truck, Louisa's truck, only moving forward now, idled up, old Og behind the wheel. He pulled to where Si used to park. Where we'd parked after.

"So I got her up, covered her with a bedsheet. Mama wouldn't talk. Si gave her whiskey on ice, and we drove to Saint Vincent's."

Og spotted us, was toting something down the overgrown path, heading our way.

"After. We drove out to Mary's Majestic. Frank, he was shit-faced. And he couldn't quit blubbering, saying my mother's name and how he'd make it all up to her. He, Frank, made me a little balsa wood car once that won a soapbox derby in Cub Scouts. He was all right. We hauled him here, right here."

Louisa nodded. "Then?"

"Si laid him out, put the barrel in his ear and shot. Once. A .22 long rifle, a squirrel gun in the ear. Not a lot of blood. We wrapped him in a piece of black visqueen," I said. "Took him to the dam bridge, where that smoke was."

Louisa looked at me, tilted her head a little. She had papers on me, but not all. "You helped kill a man?" She sat there, that sentence between us.

Og gripped the thing tight at each end, out away from his chest the way you hold a pit viper or a fish you want to look bigger in a picture.

"Si went to Tucker, and I went to Our Lady's. Other places. That's that. That's it."

"We got you fixed," Og said. "And I forgot about this. Come by parcel post. I don't remember shit."

I said, "Louisa?"

And waited—like I've waited my whole life—for her to say it was okay, for a pat on the back, he had it coming, I understand, all that shit. But that's never done any good, has it? Don't fall in love with your guilt. What else, then? You watch my back, I'll watch yours?

Louisa touched Si's prosthesis with her fingers, lightly, like testing a wound or shaving water.

In their hands then, the thing itself, silver framed and severe, the painted serpent of its length caught up before our faces. The thing, for a reason that escaped me then, had my name written on it. *Jacky-boy,* the red marker said, a corresponding finger pointing back through the letters.

Louisa said my name, brushed the filthy calf with an open hand, then wiped it on her chest. Her mouth open, I could hear her breath. I was afraid. I know now—fear came down on me then.

She started to speak, and I still picture her like that—about to say words that wouldn't come.

This remains a strange land to cross, let me tell you. Add it up any way you like, throw in love or take it away. Maybe I'm finally shit-house crazy. The southland of the heart, fire, nightmare, blood and water, all that and more. My mother's old man, long dead, told me to commune with my future self. Why not? Such communion, wouldn't it traverse a space inhabited by those beasts our minds make? So warped but hopeful, why shouldn't our selves reach back for our selves? Must we lose all?

Og said, "Here."

My flinch, instinct, the way a hand gets thrown up in front of a night fire, no shield for heat or light.

ORATORY

Jack Smith worries a sore inside his mouth, watches Louisa flip into a turn at the deep end where the boards are. Into her mile, she sprawls under the pale water for six, seven meters, then ruptures it, a fierce butterfly. *God,* she can swim. This, Easter weekend. They are alone inside the natatorium of the college where Jack lectures. Outside, the deserted campus is delirious. Dogwood ignites the blue sky. But this building was built before the war; it is dim, and the air smells like onions seized up from root dirt.

Jack has hidden himself behind the aluminum bleachers that are piled against a long windowless wall. From where he crouches, he can hear the squelched slaps of his wife's rhythm on the water. She whales into another flip, stretches against the pool floor with amazing grace. Louisa's hands, far in front of the glint cast from her green goggles, lace together—prayerlike.

He was writing a death notice when they met.

The year Jack dropped out, got his nose broken, and took a job writing obituaries at the *Democrat* in Little Rock.

He made five dollars an hour typing formal obits, phoned in from homes around the state. People died everywhere. He fielded calls from Texas, Louisiana, Idaho, Tanzania, announcing the departed who had roots in Arkansas but had passed on strange soil.

Late in the afternoon, when people had manners enough to quit dying, Jack handled Washington press releases. Louisa was a congressional aide for an Arkansas man named Mayfield that year. She called the *Democrat* that day to dictate a press release from the Capitol Hill office. The switchboard operator put the call through to Jack's desk.

"Name?"

"Louisa for Mayfield."

People lived their whole lives, died all day, got killed in car wrecks, were Rotary members, Masons, Lutherans, carpenters' wives, truck drivers, preceded in death, sisters, brothers, husbands. "Louisa Mayfield? Who?"

"Louisa." The woman's voice.

"Go ahead."

"To whom am I speaking?"

"Jack," Jack said. "Jack Smith." He could hear background office noises: a phone ringing off the wall, Xerox, voices.

"I don't know you."

"I'm in obits."

"Prove it."

Jack read from the top of the pile. "James Daniel Tucker died Sunday. He was a Baptist." His shift was from two in the afternoon until ten at night. Holidays were hell. Suicidal. "Tucker, twenty-four, of Lonoke, was a graduate of Ouachita Baptist University in Arkadelphia. You want some more? I do press too."

Louisa said no. She told him to hold, then began dictating a story about how Mayfield's constituency in Hope, Arkansas, had loaded two Volkswagen-sized watermelons onto a flatbed truck and had them hauled up to the front steps of the Capitol. Congress was issued plastic knives, carved them up right there, and ate every bite down to the rinds.

T-shirts with HOPE MELONS printed in big pink letters across the chest were issued. Everyone wore them, chomping seed, chewing. Jack pictured it, sweet juice going sticky in the afternoon sun, hot August, fragrant sun on summered legs, skin, light. He was lonely, terribly so.

"Guess what Congressman Mayfield said. My boss. Your elected rep. Are you listening? Guess?"

Out of habit, Jack had typed everything Louisa had told him into the form of an obituary—here was a structure, order-logic, hierarchy. He looked at what he'd written.

"What'd he say?"

"'Nice melons.' He pointed at my tits. He referred to my breasts as melons. What's with you people down there?"

"I'll kill him."

Louisa said, "I already did. Write me a letter, Smith. We'll correspond. I know you're a maniac. Are you a maniac?"

Jack said, "I'd like that."

Just like that. Out of a zillion days, one moment rockets toward you when fire flies.

Five years; they wrote each other letters for five years.

Jack holds a finger to his throat, times his wife by heartbeat; she is under forty from one end to the other. He's no match for her in the water. Louisa swam for the University of Maryland and just missed the Olympics in '80. She holds state records in South Carolina, has been cited in *Sports Illustrated*. Inside the locked baby room at home—she has made it into a shrine for lost things—three scrapbooks are filled with medals, ribbons, certificates of honor. One, dedicated to the trials, has a flattened paper bag taped to a page; inside, fine blonde hairs curl. Swimmers shave all over. "Guess where *this* came from?" is Magic-Markered on the page margin where blue letters have slightly smeared. Jack put a pinch of Louisa's shavings—delicate as a newborn's—into the family Bible for good luck.

Louisa is nearly six feet tall, and it's hard to tell her sex from here. She could be anyone. Her weight buoys her, allows her speed. In his head, Jack practices what he has come to do and is bewildered by this ritual from which he is excluded. Grieving, she is a passionate blur, very much alive in a black one-piece, goggle eyed, as he crouches, stripped to his underwear, behind the aluminum bleachers. He takes one last bolt of damp air as Louisa breaks into a hard freestyle, swimming straight in the middle lane. Jack crawls out on his hands and knees—like an animal, he thinks—to the ledge where FIVE FEET is chiseled into cement. Almost no sound, he lowers himself into the lukewarm water and sinks down so that his nose is just above the surface. His urine is warm. It rises in fingers against his chest as he waits for the one he has loved to swim back through the shallows.

From how many mirrors have you stolen my face? Who has given you the explanation of my failings? Do you use my tongue for a lie or a prayer?

This, what Louisa mailed after the jobless year, her panhandling spring, her *downtime,* the year when things fell down and each letter held some reference to the holes in her life. By 1983, Jack had quit his newspaper job and moved to Fayetteville, where he tried to finish the degree he'd lied about having in a résumé. He was living with a forty-year-old woman who'd advertised room and board in exchange for work, but what he mostly did was drink whiskey with her and hear the endless story of how she'd had oral sex with the Episcopal priest before Holy Communion, how her husband had gotten himself killed in a highway crash, how sleeping with her sixteen-year-old son was no longer possible because he'd started getting erections. She watched him rake out her gravel drive, stack hay head high in the loft, polish the panel walls, the banister on the stairs, all the way to her bedroom. Vague references brought immediate responses from Louisa.

People from Arkansas lived in places named Smackover, for God's sake. Louisa prodded, sometimes writing whole passages in the bumpkin dialect she'd picked up from Mayfield's home people on the Hill. For his part, Jack drafted and redrafted each letter, longhand cursive on rag paper. He sent Louisa lyric poems, self-interviews, and even wrote a story about what would happen when they met. The narrative prophesied a church wedding, how the small beads on Louisa's white dress would look as light filtered through stained glass, how she would laugh at the instant when he said, "I do."

Here is what I want you to do tonight instead of screwing your keeper, Louisa wrote on the onionskin page of a letter she claimed to have panhandled stamps for. She had enclosed a charcoal nude of herself—the only likeness Jack Smith ever knew of her until the day they met—along with a joint, "good hooter," she called it. *I want you to put on your best suit of clothes, comb your hair straight down, and perfume yourself with your best cologne. Turn the lights out and pull down the stained shades. Shut the doors. Lock them inside out. Tape me to your headboard and burn a candle close enough for the light to flicker, to jump across my contours, my roughness. Light the joint, smoke until your head swims. Let me come alive for you. Touch my paper heart, harder, smear me with two fingers down to there, see how I take you, how your fingers print me. Strip, slowly, one garment at a time as you must for a lover. See how I look you in the eye and shiver. Shut your eyes and feel my kiss on your lips, my tongue in your mouth, in the hole where you miss a tooth. Feel me cup the small of your back and listen to how my breath quickens, then stops. Blow the candle out, cover yourself with the thin sheet, see us love. Rock with me. Remember. Who to say no?*

From this level, Jack can hear the sharp exhale and inhale she makes on every third stroke, see that his great-grandmother's wedding band is missing from her left ring finger. Louisa wears no bathing cap. Her blonde hair is darkened by water and slicked back over the crown of her head, so that it looks even shorter. Jack holds a breath. He has the sensation of being half in and half out of himself. Louisa is swimming in his direction now, lurching in the backstroke that makes her vulnerable, blind to the distance between her and the wall she must use to flip. A bubbly wake skeins out behind her, fine as the lace wedding train that caught and ripped as they guided each other away from the pulpit. Jack wants to warn her of her progress, to caution against the concrete that could break a finger, arm, split her skull. He restrains himself, and, at the last possible second, as if she has some inborn knowledge of the invisible thing that she's up against, Louisa spins into a perfect flip, blooms under the onion-scented water.

They met at the foot of a neon cross, one breathtaking Easter Sunday morning on the last day of March, just as a ragtag group of worshipers kneeled to pray for the souls of astronauts. Louisa had flown from D.C. to Tulsa International, rented a car, and driven to Fayetteville, where she intended to hand deliver their fiftieth letter. Mount Sequoyah, which overlooked Fayetteville, Arkansas, the town Louisa referred to as *Fateville,* was the site of a Pentecostal church camp with some wacky NASA connection. Loud icons were situated in the blind spots of every sharp curve to surprise sightseers on the scenic route. White-faced Mary wore red lipstick; Jesus was rigged with a tape that repeated, "I am risen. I am risen," as if surprised by this stroke of good fortune. A slight wind stirred his purple robe, stained with chicken blood or some such. Jack chose this place because one could make out church steeples dazzling the valley below, how the glass covering the swordlike hands of the courthouse clock blazed; Louisa would be able to see Jack's own tin roof, how the foothills knuckled into the Ozarks toward Missouri.

As a tall, black-headed man offered up the words to the Lord's Prayer, a silver car rolled to a standstill on the road above. Jack's heart accelerated as the engine got killed and the woman he'd revealed his most private secrets to stepped out into the strong sunlight. She threaded her way through the kneeling Pentecostals, come to the neon cross for the prayer of resurrection, touching the shoulders of three younger men so that their eyes flung open as if shaken from dream. The flesh-and-blood Louisa ran circles around any charcoal nudie. She was something to see. Tall, she carried herself with the conviction of one who comes from someplace important, bearing integral news. Her hands. Look at them, see how the fingers curl, bend, flex as she writes, marks the hard $\mathcal{J}$'s loop into the flowing $\mathcal{S}$. The thumb and index fingers come together, hesitate, before the stamp is lifted, touched to the taste-bud tongue, the sweet spot blown dry. Jesus. The eyes he'd once smeared on coarse paper looked straight through him, knew and knew and knew him, discerned him by elimination, were brimful of knowing. How can you say it? Where do words go? She was close enough to breathe, to taste, to be.

One at a time, she'd brought their eyes open, nodding when they shook their heads no. Jack sat cross-legged on green grass, just beyond the stone benches that formed a crude perimeter around the blinking cross. He wore cotton, razor creases, had bounced a check on a bottle of Wild Turkey 101. He lit a cigarette, sucked teeth, fought with his coward self.

"Are you *him*?" She wore bracelets. On her wrists, they sang.

Jack said he was. He stood, shook, said, "Here."

"Good," Louisa said. She placed a wine bottle beside his liquor and kissed the side of his face. She smelled like nothing he knew. "How long does it take not to be lost around here?"

He'd rehearsed what seemed stupid now. "You're lost?"

The sun hit her skin when she took off the jacket. The Pentecostals were used to this sort of thing. "All goddamn morning. Do they have a john up here?"

They sat together beside a bench, two people.

Louisa said she could wait. "They screwed my directions from Tulsa. I had breakfast with a trucker who just knew and knew how to get me here. What is it with truckers?" She lifted arms, palms up. "I'm here. Tell me why?"

"Happy Easter," Jack said. "Any other trouble? How was your trip? My father's a truck driver."

"You never said that. You told me he owned land."

"Right. It just moves. Drink?"

She said, "Yes I would, Smith. Please. A little."

Louisa unslung a camera, claimed it had no film, and started clicking off make-believe pictures while Jack poured. The dark-headed preacher's voice rose and fell, a cadence that held within its pitch the whole barbwired world, the rain-on-tin sound of Jack's people. His oratory was filled with ringing allusions to the LORD GOD ALMIGHTY whose heavenly mansions were cemented by the blood of the lamb.

"Cheers," Louisa said. She knocked hers back, handed the glass to Jack, then snapped a few shots of the preacher, who was leading the astronaut rendition of "I'll Fly Away." Louisa let the camera fall, clapped, closed eyes, and took sun. "These people are out of this world, Smith. Who are they?" She took off her sandals. As Jack would ever notice, her feet had the beat look of a dancer's, seemed like they'd gone places, could tell stories should they speak.

"Holy Roller campers. I'm glad you're here."

She touched Jack's shoelace with a blistered foot. "Say something that matters. I want to remember how goddamn weird this is."

"You like weird? Those letters. I keep them. We know. You never judged." The Jesus people were taking sacrament. "You're queen this week, Louisa. That's something to remember."

"Take this and remember me," Louisa said. She told Jack to shut his eyes, and he did. Then, for a minute by the clock, she touched his face with her fingers. She traced the buckle of his chin, the hawked nose, still crooked from breaking, the widow's peak high on his forehead. It was like she was blind and wanted to know him; who had ever touched his face? "Hallelujah," she yelled, only half mock, so that several of the Pentecostals glanced over at them—the wayward flock.

Jack pointed out visible landmarks, showed her the direction to Little Rock, to Petit Jean Mountain, to D.C.—the town he'd once struck out for, only to have a beer-breathed hitchhiker tell him he was crazy to run off to a woman he'd never even met. He told her about Eureka Springs to the north, where a hundred-foot-tall Christ of the Ozarks with speakers bolted inside its head drew tourists from every known place on earth. Louisa got Jack to stand up straight, arms flung outward over the city below, and took his fictional picture. They drank to what had been confessed in their letters, to risk, Wayne Coomers and the Original Sins, to the dangers of how they lied and loved. Then, Louisa slipped the fiftieth letter from her coat pocket, slit it with a fingernail.

"My dear Smith," she said, just as the air broke into a cacophony, bells on top of bells clanging up from the churches in the valley below, *Fateville*. "I have loved," Louisa said, but her voice was lost to the evangelicals' discord, shrieks, rattlesnake tongues, the singing clamor knifing up through their guts, roiled into a single noise offered up to the bare blue place where words go. Louisa lipped the words of their fiftieth letter into this sea of sound, and Jack could tell by her strong expressions that she was revealing some long-kept key to her heart. She seemed to speak of the distance love carries, how we send our hope out into the great unknown places. Years later, when he finally realized what she had tried to tell him but doubted that such a moment had ever really happened, Jack would fight to reclaim the sheer kick of the instant—when this woman who knew him to the crooked core had opened up her mouth, and out had poured glory.

Jack takes a breath, heavy air, lets his body slide down the slick wall to the pool floor, where he sits, eyes open. The chlorine burns. He has read how the voices of whales carry three thousand miles under the ocean, how they sing hello and good-bye, warnings and songs that translate into joy or love or grief. The idea of messages sent out across murky channels does not lose itself on Jack, now. Through green haze, his wife butterflies the plane that separates them.

His heartbeat quickens; Jack must choose words carefully. *Don't you dare,* he says into the water. *Love,* he manages as she passes. His voice surely sounds nothing like whale music. What Jack hears is an eerie glut, the sound that comes out of humans who've lost larynxes, who speak through amplifiers held to vocal cords. *You listen to me.* Jack says it deep in his throat, breathes water, and Louisa powers away.

She isn't listening.

Jack proposed. Still out of breath from the steep hike to a place called Flat Rock, they overlooked a bend in the White River where nude sunbathers lay glistening on rocks in the stream.

This was Louisa's seventh and final day in Fayetteville. She had carefully packed their picnic: Camembert—it reminded Jack of baby shit—bread, balled melon, and red wine for their last meal. She was to depart by afternoon. Earlier, that morning, Jack had allowed Louisa to photograph his ass while standing naked on a tree stump. In Kodachrome 400—good for light.

"Let's get married," he said.

Louisa laughed and then laughed again. The question was ridiculous. "We haven't even lunched yet, Smith," she said. "There are nude people down there."

"*Nekid*," Jack said. "Say yes."

Louisa unzipped the day pack, set out two coffee mugs. She turned the bottle into the screw until it squeaked. "You're crazy." Louisa frowned. She poured three fingers into each mug. "And I'm crazy, too."

Just then, a scarlet king snake winded its way across the rock, dragging skeins of shed skin. Louisa reached out and tore away a transparent foot length. She said, "Fine."

"Snake. Don't touch that snake."

"You think you know me." She wrapped the wispy skin around a finger; it made sound, wind in October corn. Nearby, a dove's thin whistle. Hyades would predict hard rain tonight. Buddha says *pay attention*. "Reptiles mean good luck. I've heard that."

It was a spring morning in April, in north Arkansas, on a river where people without clothes on went unashamed in the sun. That was how it seemed. What signals the holy?

"Lucky. That mean yes?"

"No."

"Why not?"

"I'm embarrassed. Yes."

Jack and Louisa drew their plans on the flat rock where a snake had crossed, interrupted by an occasional yelp from a bather who'd jumped into the current. Jack could sell his cherry bed, his grandmother's chifforobe for airplane cash to D.C., where Louisa's apartment had a room with a writing desk. He'd get a job, something that would get him on her mother's good side. He'd meet the captain, her strapping father, a three-tour destroyer boss who'd schooled at Annapolis. They'd summer at Ocracoke Inlet, the family beach house, where Blackbeard once harbored and the Atlantic was money-color green. They'd tour the Netherlands, where Louisa had friends, connections, an old lover. They'd smoke hashish, screw on soft cotton, live in Adams Morgan beside a Robowash where embassy limousines got washed by shining African men each morning. And maybe they'd say vows in the National Cathedral, where Louisa had been confirmed, a priest unlike the rough man who'd bellowed for spacemen on the hilltop.

"This is my ring." Louisa slid the snakeskin onto her ring finger, held it to a sun shaft. "Like the story you keep writing. *The Book of Lies.* Too heavy?"

"You'll giggle when I say I do." They kissed. Jack was missing two back molars. Decayed already, they got knocked out of his head in a ball game. He felt her tongue there, in the space.

"Get a load of *this.*" Louisa pointed out a pair, a couple, you couldn't tell, on a rock downstream. One was on hands and knees, and the other surged behind, head thrown back, white eyed, intent. They came together, about them the whish of the river washing past carved rock banks, toward the muddy Mulberry, where the two would twine with the Arkansas, join the Mississippi that emptied into the deep silt flats beyond the Pontchattrain in the Gulf of Mexico.

"Look at them, Jack," Louisa whispered. "They're in love." She touched him.

Jack watched it happen. Afterwards, the two—indistinguishable as twins from this distance—stood upright, holding hands on the jagged ledge; they leaped out together, caught in an arc of momentary flight.

Near the far end of the pool, where the floor drops abruptly to fourteen feet and is printed by the fingers of divers who have broken their falls, Louisa is beginning her kick. She somersaults against the wall, blossoms into the stroke that initiates a battering four-lap medley of back, breast, butterfly, and the free that will bring her sprinting home. She's haul-ass blurry—a sting in his red eye. This is what he has come for; the mourning that has blistered Louisa's mind, Jack sees, is gone now; her heart's will is to finish, to end this race she reenacts, this ritual for the child she has lost. Jack deep breathes. The outside world mirrors the morning they met—the pure pitch of peripheral prayer, dogwood ignited on unfurled tongue—and he knows the future, how they will suffer

each other in silence and Louisa's slammed-shut room will fill
and fill and fill; they will awaken and go on awakening mornings
until nothing is left for them but the long sleep under a twin
stone already set in the Solgahatchie bottom cemetery. Down
their carved names the raindrop plows. He must take hold of the
adversary. Jack heaves in one deep breath after another as
Louisa's shoulders, her big back, break the calmness. As her arms
slice air. She is near. Jack fills his lungs one last time, lets himself
coil under the water, springs forth.

He'd flown into Dulles International with seventy-five dollars, two
broken typewriters, books, poetry, a desire like great fear in his
head—*when you get lost, you come to the moon in the field, the
light all lovers soil.*

Louisa met him at the row-house door, 1705 Euclid Street
Northwest, the address he knew by heart, had written to from the
Peabody Hotel, schoolyards, lovers' beds, a jail once. He smelled
like dope, she said, like whiskey. She took, read his poetry, thought
him mad, asked if he had money, a cigarette, then made love to
him on an unmade futon that smelled like Brut.

In Washington, D.C., Louisa taught the emotionally disturbed—
eight-, nine-, ten-year-olds—at an Arlington grade school, sometimes rode the Green Line home to the Twelfth and N Street row
house, where they'd moved together, to demonstrate discipline
techniques on Jack. Evenings, nights when sirens howled, they
drank in a bathtub jacuzzi to slow horn music from a cracked
front-room speaker that Jack had wired to a pawnshop phono.
He'd been hired at a restaurant called New York, New York, where
Sinatra's version played every nineteen minutes on the dot. He
made money. They bought a car. It wouldn't start.

Their story was the strangest thing they'd ever heard.

Louisa had friends in faraway places.

On the morning after the Fourth of July, as Jack dressed for
work and sang the Hare Krishna song—a shaved-headed troupe

of them had fed out curried rice on the Capitol Mall before fire-works the evening before—a foreign voice sang Louisa's name through the intercom.

"You are the lover, no?" the thick voice said. "1215 N Street. Northwest. She wrote me to come here. See?"

Jack looked out the bay window; below, in the courtyard, stood a bull-chested man whose white face mooned up under concrete-blond hair. He waved an envelope, pointed to an invisible address, nodded.

"You a bill collector? Bill collectors go to hell."

"No, no, no. We are friends in Netherlands. Louisa, she tells me to *be* here."

Jack shuffled geography in his head, while the distant voice rattled off a story about selling belongings, making a monthlong voyage across the great Atlantic in the belly of a freighter. Jack looked down at the man who told how he had not guessed how strange this United States would be, how he only had thirty-six American left to his name, and Louisa had promised. "Please," the sweet-sounding voice said. She was the *only* soul he knew.

In his heart, Jack Smith felt kinship for this stranger who'd sold earthly possessions and weathered the rough width of an ocean to be with the intoxicating voice on the other end of astounding letters. Despite the wear of travel, he was handsome, and Jack guessed him a decent man.

"There is no Louisa here," Jack said. "Go back where you goddamn came from."

For a moment, the two regarded each other, just long enough. Then Jack drew the blinds, saw how the lost Dutchman walked away, slump shouldered, toward souls he'd never known—no place in particular.

Jack skipped work that morning, bought a half gallon of Old Crow bourbon, and meticulously urinated on every letter he and Louisa had ever written to each other. He tied the sour bunch together with one of Louisa's ribbons and replaced it in the cedar hope chest at the foot of their bed. Later, when she unlocked the front door, Jack was plowing through letters from six other men; he'd ferreted them out, demanded truthful testimony from each.

Jack markered slashes under subjects that rang a bell. One was an Amsterdam postmark retelling the time he'd undressed in front of a charcoal sketch. Locked the door. Smoked dope. Jacked off. Jack could hear the man speak. This was the letter he assaulted Louisa with when she asked *what in hell he was doing*.

Jack took his wedding band off, put it in his mouth, swallowed. "I'm worth thirty-five bucks now, bitch."

She threw the rancid letters in his face, and they went at it for a good while, shouted every curse they knew, they crossed the line, they said things. When the police came, Jack pretended he couldn't speak English. After dark, they made furious love on the hardwood floor amidst shards of broken glass, ripped up pissed-on letters, because it was the one thing they had left to do.

So they talked it out. Outside, where sirens bleated on alphabetical streets, exquisitely made-up transvestites helped prostitutes apply rouge, and dealers said *number four, number four*.

Jack knifes under the shallow water. A high keen whines in his ears. Volts of juiced blood rip through the veins in his outstretched arms, out through his forked fingers. His nails seem sparked beads, clear acetylene fire. Louisa's round shoulders churn in the corner of his eye; the whiteness of her skin flashes. His calculation is right. He can almost touch her, and if water were air, a howl would quaver the rafters.

"I loathe you. No matter what I ever say. It's true."

Louisa said it as Jack shifted gears on the U-Haul truck—"an adventure in moving"—they'd rented for the move from D.C. to North Carolina. He'd been accepted, was about to make good on his promise to get degreed. "You have no right."

Jack said, "You don't mean that." It was hot as Hades inside the un–air-conditioned vehicle. Humid air leaked through the vents.

Their twenty-footer was top heavy, and Louisa was petrified of being trapped in a hulk of burning metal. Smelling herself on fire—what would that be like? She'd dreamed it so. Jack reminded her, said that they needed to get away from the war zone they'd created. Establish an in-between place, a zone where weapons could be laid down. "Don't cut me, I won't cut you."

"I know *that*, Jack. Goddamnit," Louisa said. "You owe me. You owe me, and you know."

"What?" They were in Carolina. FIRST IN FLIGHT, the sign said.

She said, "I loathe you."

"Me too."

And they drove on that way, the tall truck teetering on asphalt so hot the tire treads printed the pavement.

Now, he can see her wrinkled palms, the white goggle strap that constricts her head, how the dark suit crawls up the halves of her bottom. She's fast. Jack kicks through the last foot, dizzy, noise in his head. He can see the tiles on the far wall, how the filtered water jets out from the eyeball fittings.

Hands, claws on her throat, the skin of their dream, Jack Treadwell Smith sees his brother Jimmy, the velvet-cushioned head, crushed beyond belief, then photo-reconstructed, a whiff of cleansed skin, the hollow chest, a blue hand and sick flowers, men and women with chicken stuck in between their teeth saying how time would heal—*how to struggle free*, claw himself deckside, how to breathe again?

North Carolina. They rented a house on a street named Vista, grew tomatoes, peppers, crookneck squash, walked in the evenings, got a dog, made peace, saved, spent weekends on the Outer Banks, where cross-eyed folk spoke cockney English, and forgot. Louisa worked at a high school, was a swim coach, directed prom proceedings. Jack plowed straight through his master's and got a job lecturing history. They prepared a room in the big rent house for the child whose conception had brought showers of bright-blue baby things from well-wishers. This time. All be joyful this time.

We dress our dead too carefully is what Jack thinks at the moment when they intersect, his mind split—bloodied by lack—so that half of him desires nothing more than to see the woman float on the pool floor and the other part desperately wanting to touch her and say his love as he never has before. *This is what we come toward always,* hands on her neck, her face, their one face hot.

Six days have passed since the last love letter Jack would ever allow in his mailbox. He retyped it—a dainty envelope from Colchester, Vermont—into the form of an obituary, taped it to the head of the bed where Louisa slept. The bitter fight that erupted afterward ended when Louisa miscarried. She locked the roomful of baby things from the inside, wrote *I am a Fool* on the door with black marker. They blamed each other for the day they met, for the idiotic naïveté that had urged them to marry.

They wished each other dead.

Jack tried to drive all this from his head as he drove to the pool today, where his keys still hang in the door's lock, where he hid himself behind the bleachers, where he's watched her spin into tight, predictable flips.
  This is where she mourns her dead. Jack dreams, turning loose, *dear god, she swims.*

His eyes are open to the brilliance of an azure sky, where Louisa's gentle face hovers just above his own, her hands, her fingers, in his mouth. She's dragged him out into the open air.
  One. Two. Three. She keeps counting. Her lips, human lips. *Seven.* On his mouth. Everything's okay, everything's okay. Her words go inside him. *Eight.* Through his mouth.
  His body is someone else's. He smells flowers, Louisa's skin, honeysuckle in the gutter, vomit.
  Why are you here? She's putting her fingers in his mouth,

training his tongue away from the roof. He hears *Jesus*, then *fuck.* Words on top of words.

Over Louisa's shoulders, the belfry clock on top of bright Founder's Hall. Again. The world is newly deformed.

She kisses him, slight wrinkles at the corners of her mouth, says *wake up wake up wake up.* What in Jesus are you thinking?

His feet touch the deep clover where Louisa has dragged him. Cardinals make a ruckus in a nearby dogwood that quivers in white-hot flame, unconsumed.

I drowned you. Something like *I drowned you* comes out of his mouth. Jack's eye sees her eyes.

Louisa pounds his chest—hollow wallops, end-stopped lines, each a revolution. She's pounding his chest with both fists flying the color of big beautiful lips. *Shut up. Shut up. Shut up.* She says, "Goddamn you, breathe. Take breaths."

The sound, rasped *s*'s, articulate razors, who to say no?

I said breathe.

SIGHTINGS

Jack gets told his future life at Blind Harry's, a bar down Vista that doubles as a laundry. Sunday is free beer by the glass for members, but it's still too early not to feel guilty for being semihappy. They're folding whites, butterflying underwear into piles.

"Sane people don't decide where to move by throwing darts at a map." Louisa triple folds against her chest. She says, "Watch it." He's on number four.

Jack says, "We're packing. You told me Texas."

Teaching contracts have gone unsigned. What remains: Louisa has volunteered to be special education representative for her high school's junior/senior prom. Somehow, they've donated their truck to haul the Stairway to Heaven.

"Give me a quarter, Jack. I want to weigh."

He fishes his pocket, and it's 1990—last year. Then, it was still okay to live in a bungalow where yellow roses grew up a front porch that overlooked porticoes and Florida rooms on the wealthier side of Vista. "Here. This's a good year."

Louisa plucks the coin. "It's a quarter."

"Go first." Louisa puts the money in for him. "I think you've lost."

Sol, her name for the ancient stand-up scales, tells weight and future. Louisa's is always cheery: she's "the sunshine of someone's life," or "the seeds she's planted on life's rocky shores will bear lovely fruit." Sol hates Jack to the core, sees blackness in his heart, once told him that he should resist Satan, flee from him.

Only not today. He's about to receive a great, good gift, Sol says. "Jesus," he says. "Look."

Louisa ignores him, steps on the machine, says "Geronimo." Jack hears her money hit bottom. "Listen," she says, in a voice that sounds like divorce, "I'm pregnant. This time's a charm."

"*Sol* said that?"

Her eyes are wide—radio telescopes zeroed in. "No. I did. I've known for a while."

She's planned this, Jack understands. Folding each other's clothes, the whole day will always be part of what he's just been told. He doesn't want to be a father, believes that he will be this time. He says, "Beautiful," tries an embrace that goes out of kilter.

"Be happy, Jack. Please. For us."

Their kiss is from the moon. Jack pictures himself grown young, the fair, Lonoke, Arkansas, his mother. They hold hands, she cries. In dirty sawdust, lit by neon, she explains to him that his father, "Daddy," she says, has left them, has moved off to the Space Coast in Florida, and he won't be coming back. All his life, he's loved angry women. Cotton candy and sawdust mingle with the barker's shrill bawl, caught up in an icy October that is remembered for what is missed. Now, with Louisa, he hangs on hard—what he knows of love.

"*We're having a baby,*" Jack announces to the drinkers inside Blind Harry's.

Someone says, "*Hooray.*" A pair of arm wrestlers take their match away from the bar, where two shots of house bourbon are stood. A heavy hand slaps Jack's back, and—out of the blue—

someone produces a stale cigar in an "It's a Boy" wrapper. Jack
lights up, smokes.

Louisa says, "I want this time to be right."

"Why didn't you tell me?"

"I just did."

They tap plastic cups. "To the three of us," Louisa says.

That second, two African men, Jack's neighbors, limousine
drivers, walk through the double doors. They smile. Jack nods at
them, says, "I'm pregnant."

One man offers to shake, then judges the moment private.

"Us," Louisa says. "We're a *we* now." She slides her whiskey his
way.

As Jack tastes the hard-sweet liquor, she throws in "Let's finish
folding, babe." And that's what they do.

In the dark, Jack knows his rent house by heart. From their bedroom, where Louisa prefers the wall-window side and an extra
afghan, to what used to be their dining room is nine strides
through two doorways. A right there takes him into the kitchen,
where a wall phone hangs; over the metal sink, a picture window
looks out onto the backyard, where a horseshoe pit has gone to
grass. From here, Louisa has spied his workings in the garden
plot's clay soil—setting a Purple Hull trellis, sprinkling Sevin on
head-high Big Boys, poisoning cutworms that burrow into squash
stems. Once, she saw him exhume a Smirnoff miniature from a
lettuce bed soon to bolt; she shook her head, frowned. He once
convinced her that the ancient Greeks often made love in their
newly sown fields, they gave each crop a dose of that good dance,
blessing future yields with their best selves. They warded off
blight, nematodes, and blister beetles that year under a honeyed
moon where Carolina hard pack cushioned their knees, their
faces. An August mosaic virus was powerless against what love
had made vigorous.

From the picture window to the front door is thirty-three
strides. He crosses the hollow place where hardwood conjoins
with a weak floor joist. Under the couch, his grandfather's

.30-ought six—it hasn't been loaded in twenty years—is kept. It is his custom, on nights like this, to take the heavy gun from its case, polish the fine lens on either end of the three-to-nine scope, smell the bolt oil, the wood stock, hear the fine *click* the safety makes when turned off. The gun feels good in his hands, it's substantial, means something, ties him to his past, his mother's father, dead deer hung up under frosted red leaf, pine needles, and the sound of walker dogs baying down Bayou Meta.

Robed, he steps out the front door onto the porch. It is a clear night. A cedar plant nearby makes him think of home, wood smoke, fireplace grates, Christmas in Arkansas. Tonight, he cranks the scope to the ninth power, takes aim on the triangular Hyades, which follows the Seven Sisters and can predict rain. Swinging across the ecliptic, he sights Mizar and Alcor, two of three binaries that, to the naked eye, appear to be one bright star in Ursa Major's kink. Bright Mars has risen, rivaling twin Antares; higher in the east, he can make out the dim beginnings of Lyra's harp. The moon grows fat. Cars pass, dogs bark, who cares? Above, lion and goat drag him into summer, fiery rightness, the horse's mouth, order. He's going to be a father. As Aldebaran, a red giant, Taurus the bull's gleaming eye, enters the scope, Jack freezes. Hung in the air, a hoarse scream bleats, thins, then goes quiet. Framed in the next-door bay window, drawing light, a man, one of the limousine drivers who share his street, looks up the rifle bore, then disappears. Sirens howl off on Walker Avenue. It is a moment when the sight of another human seems the most alien thing on earth.

Jack unshoulders the gun. He says, "Sorry. The sky," but nobody's there. He waves, says, "Excuse me." What he wants is to tell the man that he's not dangerous, that standing on your porch with a high-powered rifle could be easily explained. He wasn't about to shoot anybody. He was looking at stars. It was Sunday night. Why not?

Rifle stowed, Jack takes a shot of cooking sherry and hurries to bed. He half expects a siren, cops. His mother once told him that other people see us the way we see ourselves. *The way we see ourselves,* he thinks, and imagines a child quickening toward vision—a *catastrophe?*

"Louisa. Christ," he says, in bed. She's dead still, breathing. "I love you," he says into her back.

By the next Friday—Louisa's prom day—they've chosen names: Anna for a girl, Jack for a boy, though—to the father to be—that name seems loaded: *don't jack me around, ain't got no jack, jack of all trades, jackass, jack-o'-lantern, jack off, jack be nimble, don't know jack*—all that, more. They have appointments with doctors, emergency phone numbers, lists of wholesale maternity outlets, and a real estate agent who is searching for a starter home, something with a low down. Jack has ripped down the U.S. map—a strange dartboard where three states have tiny holes in them suitable for viewing an eclipse. He's started a new résumé, applied for unemployment.

This is a cool May afternoon. Louisa is in good humor; the prom has her thinking in terms of color. She still wears the clothes from her school workday—a red cotton blouse that lightens her eyes and the sterling fish earrings Jack bought on a Cape Lookout beach trip. The nice glasses are out. A checkered tablecloth is draped over their flimsy picnic table. Honeysuckle blooms between their house and the lot where two stretch limousines—a black one and a white one—shine beside a pile of scrap wood. Two dogwoods over there have gotten in front of the sun and show off. May is a fair month in North Carolina; even the worst-kept places go crazy with azalea, crepe myrtle, electric dogwoods in bloom on every plot. Inside, a flank steak marinates for Jack's meal alone.

"I'll go six. Make that seven," Louisa says. Their game of two-handed spades has turned Jack's way. "But I know you're bluffing. Take this." She tosses out the eight of clubs, looking to ferret out a face card.

Jack takes the trick with a ten, the next three with high hearts. "When will you come home?"

Louisa's smile shows teeth long ago corrected by braces, a mark of real riches where Jack's from. "You cheat," she says, then pours watered-down wine deep into a glass. "But I've got your ass, now." The ace of diamonds skitters over the blue-patterned cloth.

"Yours," Jack says, throwing low. "Will you dance with the principal?"

Louisa throws her highest spade. He has her set. "You're jealous," she says. "Look at me. You think I'm going to the prom to fuck someone?"

A blue jay with something in its beak lands in the honeysuckle. Louisa is playing chauffeur to a black boy named Terrence, a profoundly learning disabled senior who has never been to a dance in his life. "I hope not. Not with Terry around," he says, plays the trump ace.

Louisa turns her remaining cards face up, sips her watery wine, then throws back the entire glass. "Damn you," she says. "*Damn* you."

"Read them and weep." Jack turns up all spades.

Louisa pushes her bench back, stands up straight against the table so that the sun is strong in her face. "You win, okay? But don't play that daddy thing. I *need* tonight. It's important. Don't give me shit about Terrence."

Jack says, "I know. But after midnight that truck turns into a pumpkin. Stairway to Heaven or not." His fingers feel thick; cards flit off the table when he shuffles.

Louisa braces herself, reaches down to remove a pebble that's gotten into a slip-on. "Come zip me when I call."

The jay makes an angry noise from the shimmering thicket, shakes whatever it's got a hold of from side to side. Jack says, "I'll miss you," but his wife has disappeared into the house. Inside, he hears closets, chest of drawers opening and shutting. He imagines how the long black gown will look against her skin, against the firmness of her thighs, how the string of pearls will seem gauzy around the thinness of her neck. What will Terrence's family think when this pale woman, tall, blonde, smelling of gestation, taps on their screen door to usher the touched son toward a night whose theme is the Stairway to Heaven? Will traces of Louisa's new motherhood tarry with them long after the truck has retaken the highway? It occurs to Jack that he should cross the fence line, rent a by-god limousine, give her the works on such a night. Their own truck's dented fender—passenger side—is a reminder of his night driving. It should be hammered out, he thinks, adding up the score to their unfinished game.

Behind the bedroom's wide-open blinds, Louisa's voice lilts. "I'm waiting," she says. "Jack. I'm *waiting* on you."

After a tough steak in front of the bedroom television, he misses the final *Jeopardy* question—*behave as you wish others to behave is the basis for this German philosopher's "Categorical Imperative."* The half-packed house feels vacant already. Jack sweeps the kitchen. Before he knows it, he's worked his way out onto the front porch, down the steep steps where one unusually high tier has necessitated a DANGER sign. Beer bottles, acorns, and scraps from unpaid parking tickets have gathered between the sidewalk and their ivy-covered bank. Next door, one of the limo men has taken tonight off; Jack hears horn music—a clarinet, Benny Goodman, maybe. A gust from the wealthier side of Vista carries the scent of basil, good bread, and extra-virgin olive oil; someone's grilling fish.

When the limo man opens his front door, Jack's broom gets away from him. It whacks a porch board, clatters down the steps. "You," he says.

The room behind the man is a replica of Jack's—down to the fireplace bricks, only different. Beside a rocking chair, an end table is set with a vase of yellow dog roses, Louisa's favorite. Jack says, "I'd like to talk to you. If that's okay, sir."

"Sir?"

Woodwinds whistle from invisible speakers. Jack retrieves the wayward broom, rests both hands on its butt. "My wife's gone to a prom. You guys see a bunch of those? I almost walked over and rented you tonight."

"Rented me?"

"For my wife. She's a teacher. Her prom's tonight."

"What'd you come here for?"

"The other night," Jack says.

The man's hands are bronze, they flutter, and a cigarette appears. "The other night what?"

Jack stands in the doorway. "It's never loaded. I mean, I'm just looking at stars."

"Are you talking to me?"

"I'm trying to say. When you saw me point my gun, I wasn't pointing at you."

"I saw you point a gun at me?"

"Sunday night."

"You're my neighbor, right? Am I some other black man? You think we all look the same, huh?"

"You saw me through the window. Looking at the sky." Jack says, "My wife's taking some kid to the prom tonight."

The room is silent for the moment between musical arrangements. "Your wife's pregnant. Don't talk to me about her." The man's words are smoke, they hover between them.

Jack notices that the fireplace is decked out with glass instead of screen. "The kid has a learning disability."

"Why are you here? You have a disability?" He sits in the ribbed rocking chair so that Jack's facing him from the doorway. "Talking about pointing a gun some goddamn where?" His mouth shows silver, gold in places way back.

Jack asks his name.

The chair rocks slightly forward; it grates against the hardwood. He says, "Witherspoon."

Jack says, "Mr. Witherspoon?" Light falls, Jack's shadow bends in front of him. A different music has started, slower.

"You should watch out whose door you knock on."

Time is running out. "See, I use the gun scope as a telescope. I don't even own shells."

Witherspoon flicks a long ash into his free hand, nods. Louisa has claimed that she will not raise a child in a house where liquor coexists with a .30-ought six. She likes to say it; *thirty-ought-six,* she says, one hard syllable at a time. "A telescope," Witherspoon says. "Your point?"

Jack says, "Nothing."

He offers to shake. To Jack's surprise, Witherspoon stands, walks to the door, shakes hands firmly. He says, "Later on, hoss."

Then Jack picks up sweeping where he stopped and works his way back home. Between houses, he uncovers a name written into the concrete; he sweeps up the high steps, past the DANGER sign, which now seems charged with the formality of a joke.

Hoss. The man had called Jack "hoss." What the hell was hoss?

Jack spends the rest of his Friday night alone, sipping red wine and calling the emergency medical numbers that Louisa has magneted to the refrigerator door. No, it is not urgent, he says. Yes, he has had a nip or two. Yes, they *are* having a baby, and he does have questions. No, it's *not* the first time. Two nurses from the all-night hot line hang up on him before he gets a talker. Her name is Cindy, and she does not mind that he's a partly plowed man with poor, poor telephone manners. Cindy assures him that everybody gets cold feet somewhere along the line, that North Carolina's high mortality rate is nothing to fear. This telephone nurse claims that Louisa sounds healthy and emotionally stable— important traits for birthing.

"What about abortions. We've done that."

Cindy doesn't miss a lick. "Not a problem." She says, "That's a myth, cervix hardening and all that."

Jack asks Cindy how he sounds; does he sound stable?

"How old are you, sir? Let's start with that."

Jack pictures her in dress whites, craving something other than a conversation like this on a Friday night.

He says, "I bet you have blue eyes, Cindy. Do you know what this sound is?" He cracks ice into his tumbler, lets Merlot gush up to the rim. "What do you make of that?"

Cindy says, "I'm losing you here."

"I'm thirty. That's ice in a glass. How old are you?"

Jack is told he's going to have to hold. When Cindy comes back, her voice misses its earlier amusement over Jack's approaching fatherhood. "Sir," she says. "Do you have a genuine concern?"

"I do."

"Well? Shoot."

Jack asks the nurse if she's ever taken aim on the night sky or made love in a garden where whiskey was hidden. Has she ever thrown a dart at a map, hit the big heart of Texas, and been ready to flee? Did she fear what gets added and subtracted in the blood we pass down? He asks her if Witherspoon sounds like poetry, what it means when someone calls you "hoss." Finally, he says that it's late, that he's lonely, and that he's probably said too much. "I hope you haven't recorded all this," Jack says. "Am I being monitored?"

"We have you on file," Cindy says.

He wishes his best into the dead line.

What can a man do when it's after midnight, when he's under the influence, and the woman he loves—inside of whom beats his baby's heart—drives up the concrete drive and halts just beneath a backyard night-light with a Stairway to Heaven dangling red flagged off the back of his truck? Around one-thirty, Louisa does exactly that.

Jack meets her at the driver's door before she can get out. "What's this supposed to mean? Are you divorcing me?"

The thing creaks a little in the truck bed as Louisa explains how she and Terrence had helped take the prom scenery apart after the dance, how their Chevy was the only vehicle big enough to haul off the two-by-twelve staircase. "*No*, I'm not divorcing you. Are you drunk?"

"But what are *we* supposed to do with it?" Several gaudy feet of the structure hang off the truck's tailgate, where a Guilford Billygoat T-shirt is tied into a makeshift flag.

Louisa says, "I'm tired, Jack. We'll deal with it tomorrow."

"Tomorrow?"

"Goodnight. Don't be long," his wife says. "You've been drinking." At the screen door, she adds, "I love you."

When the bedroom light goes out, Jack retrieves what's left of the wine and bides his time in the back of the truck where the Stairway to Heaven glitters. Six feet wide, it has seven steps. What do you do with such a thing? Here was a ladder for a king and queen to climb, a wooden passage to the temporary land of dreamy dreams. These stairs—rough board and nail—had held the spotlight's gleam, had been a stage from which kisses were flung out to children who were hell-bent on busting from one world to another. It was heavy, would take a woolly mammoth to haul out. And, in the bed of the truck, with his pregnant wife already sleeping inside the house he'd soon be leaving, Jack tries to believe in what it takes to move upward toward what is unseen. Their life together was becoming a thing that he couldn't put his finger on—that much he knew. Jack toasts the place that will soon have him, almost prays, then doesn't.

"Why are you sleeping on the couch?" Still wet from the bath Jack's listened to her taking, Louisa falls onto the cushions beside him. They cover with a flannel sheet he's pirated from the linen cabinet. Underneath them, the rifle that Louisa won't live with points toward Vista Street—toward open road. This morning's air is chilly, and Louisa's embrace feels like a mother's arms.

Jack says, "I can't sleep."

"All that red wine." Louisa's hair is catching light; its wet length seems silver. "You shouldn't leave us alone. We thought you'd got lost."

Dim sun filters into the living room, where odds and ends from their life together stack against the walls. A bar stool, a legless coffee table, and boxes with *Christmas, Wedding,* and *Glass* take up space. A beanbag chair leaks beans, and Monopoly money is scattered from a disputed game. "How was prom night?"

Louisa rubs a long, new-shaven leg against his shins, touches his ankle with her toes. "Terrence wore a top hat. He kept saying 'marvelous this' and 'marvelous that.' His father waited up on us."

Jack says, "Marvelous," and doesn't like himself for saying that.

Outside, in light Saturday traffic, the neighbors' limousines are being warmed for trips to and from the airport. What kind of person needs to be driven that way at such an hour?

"Are you hung over?"

"Ask me something else."

Louisa cradles her stomach's midripple. "You *are* hung over."

"I need a job," Jack says. This close, his wife's face is huge, a pale sky crisscrossed with lines that shift; he's never learned to read her. "Maybe I'll start a hot line for fathers. Tell them what they're getting into."

"Like you know." Louisa grips his underwear with the toes of her left foot—a trick he's forgotten. She moves on top of him, pushes his bare back down into a rough cushion. "Tell me what you're getting into?"

He says, "Now?"

Louisa rocks forward, exhales mouthwashed breath in his face. "What did you do last night? While I was dancing?"

"Do we have to talk?" Jack says to the nipple of one swaying breast.

Through a front window, sun's in the treetops. The birds are kicking into gear, making a loud, high ruckus in the neighborhood. They sing out across Vista Street and beyond.

Jack shuts his eyes.

"No talk then," Louisa says.

After, she says, "Thanks a lot." Louisa kicks the flannel sheet to the floor, stands up, stretches in the milky light. Her back cracks as she windmills side to side, throwing shadows. "I should've let you sleep."

Jack says, "It's Saturday morning. Tell me what you're talking about."

Louisa's heels thump hollow wallops as she walks out. When she returns, an empty half-gallon jug glistens; Jack watches her cram a yellow corsage into the wine bottle's mouth. "Here," she says.

Still dizzy from sex, a flower-studded wine bottle is the last thing in hell he expects. "Jesus. Where did you come from? We just made love."

Naked, his wife seems more dressed than anyone he's ever been accosted by. "You think the world owes you something, Jack. You think everyone owes you a pat on the back."

"Is this hormones?"

"I'm *glad* I'm pregnant, Jack. Do you *understand* that? Do you understand for one fricking second that you're part of this?" Louisa touches herself just above her belly's tan line, then waves a hand at the belongings they've packed in boxes. "And I'm glad we're not moving to bullshit Texas."

Jack says, "Or Utah, or Massachusetts. There were three places."

The vein in Louisa's forehead has gone purple—she means business. Once, when the sewer clogged, the neighbor's waste bubbled up through their own toilet. For a solid week, whenever they flushed, the neighbor's excrement flowed up into Jack and Louisa's bathroom. Finally, Louisa screamed, "I've had all your shit I'm going to take. Fuck your shit," she'd hollered, barreling out into the front yard, fist clamped. He'd been convinced entirely that she'd fight *anybody anytime* and *win* if the situation necessitated. Louisa says, "Those are lousy states, too."

The sugary wine smell mixes with the odor of flower. He says, "Let's don't screw the morning up."

Louisa retrieves Jack's boxers, wipes him off her. The underwear flutters over the *Christmas* box. She says, "I'd sure hate to screw up your morning. I'm sorry." But Louisa's about to soften, it seems, when they see.

In front of the house, a stretch limousine idles low where their walk joins Vista's asphalt sheen. The front-door panes fog. "Get a look at this," Jack says.

Witherspoon walks into their line of sight; dressed in dark blue, his white gloves seem made of papery radiance—membranes of light. "Maybe we should rent it," he says. "Celebrate." Jack pushes the front door open, and they stand there, Louisa behind him, taking in the polished car that seems to take up a world of street.

Louisa says, "Limousines are tacky, Jack. Do you think it has a television?"

He can feel her skin, her breasts against his back. "I bet he's got champagne in there. Enough to last clear to Hatteras." Before Jack can finish speaking, Louisa is gone. His back goes cold. Moving away, he hears her say, "*God.*"

Witherspoon walks like a man about to get into a limousine. Jack says, "Hang on, Louisa. Watch this."

Below him, the car is deep black, the color inside a light socket. Witherspoon makes his way to the driver's-side door, opens it before standing at what looks like attention. It is as if he waits for Jack to issue a destination, to take a seat on the fine leather, light a cigar, slosh champagne into stemmed glasses, and be whisked to some place that only he knows by heart.

"Louisa?" The man is staring straight at him—through him— through the entirety of his house.

In the kitchen, far behind him, a door opens, slams shut.

"Morning, Mr. Witherspoon," he says. "Give us a lift?"

The limousine driver looks Jack up and down, turns his gaze toward the sky—clear cobalt, this morning—then looks back. He removes the fierce, blue hat, props huge elbows on the car's moon roof, and smiles a smile that shows noble metal.

"Son," he says. "You ain't got no clothes on."

Then, the heavy black door swings shut. Jack can't see him through the smoke-tinted glass. As if leading a procession, the car pulls out and drives slowly away, past the porticoes and Florida rooms across Vista, away from their driveway, where the Stairway to Heaven must be reckoned with. It passes the crusty sidewalk, where Jack swept over the names of strangers, overtakes Blind Harry's, where drinks are being served. Witherspoon moves toward the city's outer boundaries. This limousine leaves for a world where the heads of drivers—fresh from good nights of sleep—turn as they dart in and out of the endless traffic, secure in the knowledge of where they go.

"Louisa." Jack sucks air. *"Louisa?"*

She's not there.

Beyond the thirty-three strides from where Jack stands to the picture window, his wife struggles. In sweats, she's muscled the heavy staircase out onto the cement drive. The glitter's already gone, strips of still crepe paper in the garden plot. Two risers knocked off, a third in the balance. What she takes clawhammer to is unwieldy, not easily undone.

WHY I LIE

On certain nights I call my blood father, whom I've never seen. I do it while my wife and little Jack sleep by the glow of our bedroom television, when my stashed bottle hasn't been found and all the petty tasks are done in the house where we are temporary caretakers. If I've drunk enough to want company and no one's answering, an unrooted part of myself awakens; this is when I dial the Tucson number I've thrown away so many times that I know it by heart. Rita—my father's girlfriend—usually picks up. She answers my small-talk questions in her sexy voice while Ed listens on another extension, a silent subject of what we say. Lately, they have come to recognize my Arkansas slur and suspect I want money, which is not true.

"You haven't been married long enough for your wife to want to leave. You and your pop imagine things." Rita is on the line tonight, telling me how women say things they don't mean, how the fierce August heat has kept her and my father indoors for two days straight. "Is it so bad there, baby?"

I tell her we had hail this afternoon. "Big as baseballs, and Louisa saw a tornado cloud," I say, though that season is long gone. "What's Ed up to?"

My father's throat clears, a husky rasp like cardboard tearing. "Ice is holy here. People pay for it," Rita says. "This heat makes me think of things like that. Do I seem weird to you?"

"Not at all."

"Oh sure. You and your father," Rita says, disappointed. "Funny Jack, your name popped up today."

"How's that, Rita?"

"I want a kid because I've never had one. Eddie was telling me about the day you were born. How the doctor kept coming out and saying, 'The kid won't make it,' and then, 'The mama won't make it.' And the whole time these carolers are singing 'Silent Night' because it was Christmas. Ring a bell?"

"No," I tell her. "I've never heard it that way." It's quiet in this far room of the house, and the kitchen lamp throws my crooked shadow on the just-mopped floor. I finger a Polaroid of Louisa, the baby, and me, the one she once wanted to send on greeting cards. "You want a baby?"

"Sure. Who doesn't?" Rita tells me to hang on for a second. When she's gone, I'm alone with my father, listening to dead air.

My mother destroyed everything she had that was related to Ed, except me. I grew up inventing blood fathers: an Apache chief, a wizard, and John Wayne on horseback—guns blazing—all coalesced in the man I made. Once, my mother whipped me for signing *Geronimo* on the parent's line of a report card. Afterwards, she cried and said it was in my blood, that my father could make lies with his hands, with his body.

"But Eddie's fixed. He can't have any more kids." Rita's voice comes out of nowhere. "Jack, sugar, he thinks about you. Right now. He tells stories about the day you two meet."

I imagine the *stories* my father made up. When I was sixteen, someone sent him a football picture of me, dressed in the red and white of my team. It later came back to me that I'd been starting tailback for the Razorbacks, that I'd engineered a big win over Texas. "I have a son now, Rita."

"No," she says. "Tell me the truth."

"He's in bed with his mother right now."

"Why haven't you told us? Your father would die to see a grandchild."

A hiss comes over the line like kindling when fire catches. This is costing me, I think, and am about to hang up when the line clears.

"Jack? This is your *father* speaking. Don't hang up."

This was only the second time I'd heard my blood father's voice. On the weekend before I graduated from high school, Ed called my mother's house and asked O. W.—my stepfather—if he could talk to me. Ed said he was booked on a flight to Little Rock, that he wanted to make things right between us. He ended the call by saying, "I love you, son." Later, from the football field where my class was seated for the ceremony, I searched each of the well-lit faces in the bleachers for one like my own.

I say hello to my father. "How have you been, Ed?"

"Good," he says. "What's this about me having a grandson?"

"The fifteenth of January. He was over eight pounds."

"What's his name?"

"Don't worry about it," I say, and am unnerved that Louisa and I have birthed a child that is part of him. They could have each other's eyes for all I know.

"It's time I fly out and meet you guys."

"Right."

My father tells me he wants a true picture of me to take to his grave. "I want us to work on a car together or something."

"Are you sick?"

"We need a truce on this, Jack. And we won't live forever."

This is how fathers speak to their sons, I think, passing on years of wisdom and gut instinct. I say, "I'll kick your ass."

Ed laughs. "You don't mean that."

"Try me."

"Tell me this," he says. "Why do you call here?"

This is not a question I expect, and an old ache quickens at my core. "I don't know why," I say, then slam the phone into its cradle, pick up and slam home again, until pieces of the sky-colored plastic pirouette across the clean, white linoleum, out onto the dark hardwood of our family room.

Louisa shakes me awake the next morning, a humid August Saturday, saying a couple of prospects who claim to have let our phone ring off the wall are here to view the house. She says they're crazy about the place and can't wait to get a look at the master bedroom. Louisa yanks back heavy bay window drapes, sees the light hurt my eyes, then struggles with a window that is painted shut. Ten o'clock sun is loud on the yellow wallpaper; it glares on the glass face of our son's photograph, which sits on the vanity with Louisa's mother and father. When I prop against the headboard, little Jacky lets fly a gleeful yelp and comes scooting toward me in his walker. His mother lets him go mornings without clothes, and I watch my naked son come to me in the bright light.

"Tell him to get out of bed," Louisa says, swiping the comforter away from my chest. "He's mean today because last night was a D-night." My wife letters a red *D* beside the date on our kitchen calendar for each night I overdrink and make phone calls. "What happened to the telephone, anyway?"

I say, "Morning, sweetie," and lean into the sour-milk smell of Jack's forehead. When he opens his mouth, a chunk of blue plastic dribbles down his chin.

"Are you going to answer me?" Louisa spins on the balls of her bare feet, so Jackie thinks she's playing a game and puts his hands over his eyes.

I check Jack's mouth while my wife stares. "I hung up on my father. How long have they been out there?"

"O. W.? Which father?"

"Ed."

"Why are you calling him?"

"Don't you call your father?"

"That's different," Louisa says. "Coffee's on the stand." She pitches jeans and a clean sweatshirt onto the foot of our bed as Jack wobbles off toward the hall, making the happy noises I strain to keep hearing.

I ask my wife if we can be friends today.

Louisa unbuttons the third button of her blouse, faces herself in the full-length mirror, and runs a hand through her short, sun-lightened hair. "Sure," she says. "Just get those people out of here, Jack. I don't feel like it today."

"Twenty minutes and they're history."

Louisa says, "I'm counting. One, two, three," then wipes her eyes with the cuff of a sleeve and smiles a sad smile at where she sees my face in the mirror. "Chop, chop," she tells me, and shuts the door on her way out.

Louisa has sworn that if something good doesn't happen before the house sells, she'll move Jack back to Maryland, where her parents can give them a decent life. I lured her to North Carolina, then Arkansas after years of letter writing. She was an aide to an Arkansas congressman in D.C. when I was on the obituary desk at a Little Rock newspaper. Once, she called on the WATS line, and we loved the sound of each other's voices. I told her I was going to publish a novel called *The Book of Lies,* and she fell for how my letters included her in the son's search for a nameless father. But *The Book of Lies* was never finished, and my part-time teaching jobs never pay in the summer. We live rent free in exchange for showing a once-grand home across from MacArthur Park, a part of Little Rock that is run down enough to be perfect for those who can afford a tax shelter. My wife says what we're doing is no way to raise a child; I know this and am ashamed.

"You have a beautiful family," the big, red-faced man who has introduced himself as Tyler Rush tells me. His wife, Bev, is inspecting my bedroom's walk-in closet. "Cedar," she says from inside. "Can you imagine that?"

Tyler says he remembers what it's like to be young, just starting out and all. He and his wife once ate ketchup sandwiches for a solid week, he says, and winks, as if I'm supposed to understand. When Bev joins us, he says, "We want this house." Bev asks if she can try out the adjoining bathroom, and I say, "Don't fall in."

"Love at first sight," Tyler says, eyeballing the ceiling. His open mouth seems full of gold. "But it always happens fast for us. We're the Rushes, you know."

It occurs to me that this man could be my blood father, masquerading as a buyer with some woman he'd rented off the street. Have them meet like this, I think, and make a mental note for the part of my novel that never goes right. "Do you have children?" I ask, after escorting them through the front door.

"Five," Rush says, and holds one hand up, fingers splayed. "Grown and married." He can't resist testing the doorbell. When he pushes the button, nothing happens. Across the street, beyond the Rushes' white Lincoln, children play on park swings and parents monitor them, reading book snippets between glances. Tyler says, "Later on," and we shake for a moment. When he lets go, a twenty is cupped in my palm. "Today's your lucky day," he tells me. "We'll be in touch."

Bev blows a kiss from their big, moving car.

"We eat porterhouse," I say. "Every night of the week."

Louisa takes Jack to my mother's that afternoon, where she sun-bathes in the backyard and lets Grandmother take a turn at being Mom again. After Ed, my mother married and divorced my step-father three times; she had offers in between. When I was a teen-ager—O. W. off sobering in Florida—a man named Frank Bottoms proposed to her and filled our rent house with the Brandon House furniture my mother loved. It was a time when I dreamed my lost father was an astronaut whose Apollo flight made it to the moon, where he and his fellows played golf in the Sea of Tranquility. No new man could fill shoes that had tried gravity. Frank got mean, and his name—like Ed's—was never spoken in the house where my mother taught me to mix the stiff Manhattans that eased her through.

I've just ripped up my last twenty pages and am knocking out the meeting scene when Rita calls to say my father is on his way to Arkansas. I'm running on the raw energy I get after a few drinks on a hangover, and the work I've just undone has my heart beating hard. Rita's voice is a whisper across our bad connection, and I ask for a repetition of what she's just said.

"This is Rita, your *father's* girlfriend," she says, as if speaking to a foreigner or a small child. Her voice sounds far away—a tongue from the moon. "I'm calling from Tucson. Your father is on an airplane right now to meet you in Little Rock."

I jiggle the cord until our line clears but say nothing. A moment that I've not prepared for is happening.

"I'm not supposed to be telling you," Rita says, "but Eddie's heart is in this, honey. Am I getting through?"

"Yes. I hear you."

"He wants to surprise you, Jack. Why I'm calling is because he's doing a good thing. You've got to give him a chance now."

"Why?"

"It'll kill him if you don't."

I force a laugh and try to get my bearings. I'm a twenty-nine-year-old man, sitting at a table where my wife has left the glasses she'll be needing to read in the yard where my mother is treating my son like me. I'm living in a house I could lose any day; to my left, hooked on a cabinet door, is the wall calendar, where red *D*s are marked deep into many of the numbered boxes. I am the father of a son who cannot know that his mother is not happy with our lives; I am the blood son who has lied his father from hero to villain and must now deal with the real man.

"What's he like, Rita? Honest."

"Ed's a good person," Rita tells me. "He has character. He has big arms and good teeth, and he likes to cook. Your father takes care of me."

"Do you love him?"

"Yes, I love him. My Eddie's not who you think he is," she tells me in a tone that is nothing like the one we've made drunk talk in while my father listened. "He's scared of you, and I don't blame him."

"What does *he* have to be afraid of?"

"Baby, if you don't know, I can't tell you." Rita explains how my father will call my house in the morning; he'll ask to meet wherever I like, and he doesn't expect to just walk into my life empty-handed. My father has cashed in a savings account, Rita claims, and is bringing the money for my family to do with as we like. If his plan fails, at least he's tried, and she'll be there for him when he comes home.

"I never said anything about money."

"But you'll take it," Rita tells me. "I sure would."

I smoke cigarettes and drink coffee for the rest of the afternoon, pacing the house while retelling myself the old story my mother once told on a night when I was young enough to let thunder scare me into her bed. She met my father when she was nineteen—a *girl*, I remember her saying—and keen for the world outside of where she'd been. Ed had one week left at the air force base in Jacksonville, before he went back to Arizona, where his father owned a five-hundred-acre ranch where Geronimo once slept with his band of ragged braves before one last run at Old Mexico. My father carried a picture of his little girl, whose mother had been killed in a car wreck. Ed was young and tanned, and brash like John Wayne, and he offered my mother a new life with the little girl, under a sky Ed claimed was the same pale blue as his eyes. So my mother left Little Rock in a light February snow, while her father—big old Si—threw beer bottles at their moving car. They were married by a sleepy justice somewhere in the big heart of Texas. Ed's car broke down in Las Cruces, New Mexico, and they hitched to Tucson, where everything my father had said was a lie. No ranch, no little girl, none of it. I was born on a blazing-hot Christmas Day that year, in the Pima County hospital where my father was listed as unknown. Together, we left for Arkansas, where my mother's state job and, after, O. W. supported us from one rent house to the next. I remember lying in bed that night, listening to the odd bedtime story of my lineage, while the lightning lit my mother's face with violent clarity.

That night, after we show the house to a single man who is thinking of starting a rehab center for vets, Louisa gives me the first haircut I've had in three months. This is also Jack's first cut. My clippings mingle with his on a white sheet, spread on our bedroom floor, where a kitchen chair faces the television. A news bulletin has interrupted a ten-year-old's tap routine on *Star Search* and is all about how two escapees have just been apprehended near UALR and are being returned to Cummings.

"What's the occasion?" Louisa asks, scissors clacking all

around my ears like she knows what she's about. "Have you decided to get a job?"

Little Jack is crawling on the sheet at my feet, putting strands of our hair in his mouth and touching our feet. Louisa's fingers feel good on my neck, on the crown of my head. "That's too close to home," I say, as the camera pans the campus where I'll soon go back to work.

"You never answer me." Louisa forces the comb's fine end through the thick hair on top.

"I have a job."

Louisa says, "I wrote a bad check for groceries this afternoon. Will your job pay for that?"

"I think the house may sell."

"Tell me something I don't know," Louisa says. The news flash is over, and a second-round comedian wants the audience to guess what is in his hand.

"I think we may come into some money. Soon." I try to see my wife's reaction, but she straightens my head and guesses a razor blade in the comedian's balled fist.

"Are you going to sell something? Your lie book?" Louisa pulls down on the lobe of my right ear, so I hear the tear of each cut. "Or did someone die?"

"My father. Ed's in town. We're going to meet him in the morning."

"You're making this up." Louisa tells me this about the same time she gets a piece of my ear. My reflex is a backhand that sends the scissors flying across the room, one point knifing through the thin blue cushion on Jack's walker, before the other gashes a piece of baseboard on the far wall. My wife looks at me like I'm a maniac, one of the escaped convicts who ought to be shackled in solitary confinement. "What in hell are you doing?" she screams.

Jackie joins in, squalling in airless bursts that make me afraid he's choking. I finger the nick on the top side of my ear, hold my hand in front of my face, so drops of blood roll down my wrists, onto the stark sheet.

"You cut me," I say, as calmly as I can manage.

The scissors clack together when I retrieve them. Louisa has picked Jack up and is saying something to him that I can't under stand. He's still fighting for his breath, and I'm amazed at how quickly things get out of hand, how a moment you've planned out can go crazy on you.

My wife looks from the scissors to my face, then starts to cry. Inside, I'm afraid that this is it, that she'll pack a suitcase, call a cab, and I'll never see either one of them again. "You should get down on your knees and pray," she says. Her voice cuts to the quick. "If those scissors had hit my son, I'd kill you. I swear to God."

I try to say I'm sorry, that it was an accident. When I reach over to touch Jack, Louisa takes two quick steps back, says *no*.

"I know you're sorry," she says.

"What do you want me to do?"

Before she can answer, my son does something neither of us expects. A commercial on television, the one where a pink bunny marches with a drum strapped to his chest, gets his attention, and he stops crying as suddenly as he started. I'm not even sure he can see that far, but for some reason our boy starts to laugh—not exactly a happy laugh but a gibberish verging on what we both recognize as a signal that things are okay.

Louisa looks me in the eyes and shakes her head. I wonder if it was ever like this for my mother and father, if, before the separation, they had the world shift into another gear and no one laughed at the perfect moment.

"It's okay now, sweetie," Louisa says, ruffling Jack's new-cut hair with her free hand. "It's okay."

I am allowed to embrace my wife and son for an awkward few seconds, long enough to be sure they're mine again. Some of the cut hair has stuck above Jack's upper lip, so it looks like he's wearing a thin, fake moustache. Louisa kisses him on the mouth and giggles when the hair tickles her nose. I catch a glimpse of myself in my wife's vanity mirror; with half my hair cut off, I resemble two people.

Louisa says, "Can we finish?" She lets little Jack crawl onto the bed and kisses me for the first time of the day. "Or do you think you'll need stitches?"

"You just nipped me. I didn't mean to overreact."

"Good," Louisa says. "What about your father?"

My wife turns the television off, has me sit down, and pinches the small cut until blood stops. While she finishes cutting, I tell her why Ed has come to be in Little Rock, how I called him for reasons I cannot explain. I tell Louisa that I've never asked for money. It was *his* idea, I say, and try to explain how it felt when he didn't show up years earlier. Finally, I try to tell her the way I feel now, that I'm fearful of what my father will see in me, what I'll see in him. Later, as we lie in bed—our son in between us—Louisa assures me that this could be a turning point in our lives, that meeting my father as a family may be the one good break we've waited for.

"What if he doesn't show up this time?" I ask, but Louisa has turned on her other side and fallen asleep. I shut my eyes for a while and trace the soft contours of my son's face—the slight flare of his nostrils, the cleft in his chin. He does not know who I am, I think, and hang on the instant when I'll look my old man in the eyes and see what my own boy may one day find in me.

On Sunday morning, after the paper falls, the three of us dress to meet Ed. Louisa has an eye for color; she chooses an outfit for little Jack that will match the blue in my suit jacket and lays out the lavender dress she has kept under plastic since leaving North Carolina for Arkansas, where I promised to hammer out a life for us. She offers me a sip of her whiskey-laced coffee while I shave. "You don't want to cut yourself," she says, and smiles behind me in the mirror, where I've wiped a clean circle. The bathroom radio is tuned to an early morning service, and the congregation is singing the doxology to the heavy rumblings of a pipe organ. "Let me do the back of your neck," Louisa says, then shaves me, humming the last three notes while the people sing, "Ho-ly Ghost."

After dressing and spit polishing the black shoes I was married in, I try eggs Benedict—Louisa's favorite breakfast—but get the hollandaise wrong and let the eggs get overpoached before I finish.

"Are you nervous?" Louisa is pressing fresh pleats into the pretty dress while Jack amuses himself by crinkling the plastic bag in our garbage, where my first batch of bad sauce is spattered.

"No. Should I be?"

Louisa says, "You look real good today. When's he supposed to call?" She holds the purple dress up to her chest, so the hem hangs down on one of her long calves, darker after a day's sun.

"Anytime." I check out the phone by calling my mother, hanging up when she answers. She sleeps late on Sundays, and her voice is a mixture of fear and confusion. "He'll call when he calls," I say, and we eat our breakfast while tape-recorded church bells from down the street announce the call to worship.

Jacky wheels his walker around the kitchen while we eat, like he's after something only he can see. He zeros in on Louisa's dress, draped over his empty high chair; my son touches the fabric with tiny hands, brings the cloth near his face, breathes in a state that his mother has left behind.

When we've finished poring over the Sunday paper, after the breakfast dishes are done and I've sneaked an extra shot of bourbon into my coffee, the cracked phone is a silent reminder of our waiting. Louisa decides we should pose for a family picture, one to replace the thumbprinted Polaroid on display in the kitchen. I flip the wall calendar to September—I don't want to see the marks against me today—and join them in front of the big painted columns on the front porch, where the sun is strong in our faces as she adjusts her tripod and camera aperture. Louisa runs to where Jack and I wait, her short heels clicking on the sidewalk, as the camera beeps for us to smile. This moment seems ripe full of the great good luck it takes to go blindly toward what we don't know but hope for. And when the shutter's speed catches the three of us, huddling in the makeshift embrace this short time allows, I swear to slug out the long fight for what my father lost.

"Let's get one more," Louisa says, as she winds her film forward, but I explain that we shouldn't press our luck.

Ed calls at twelve noon, just as Louisa is changing Jack into clothes he can deal with. We agree to meet on the front steps of the capitol, an easy target from the hotel where he's stayed the night. My father tells me that he knows this is sudden—he's surprised himself by coming—and he won't blame me if I need more time to get used to the idea. Louisa is beside me, raising her eyebrows and nodding her head, mouthing the word *him*.

"Today's a perfect day," I tell him. "Give us an hour."

Ed says, "You don't need to get your mother in on this. Do you?"

"She won't know. Don't you ever mention her again. Understand?"

Ed says he won't say anything more about *Jackie*. This is the first time I've heard a man say my mother's given name in a while. When I was young, deep voices asked for her that way on the telephone. Sometimes I thought they were asking for me.

"Tell your cab to drop you by the capitol. Okay?"

"You sure?"

I say I'm sure.

"Have you changed since the pictures I got?" Ed claims he has a surprise gift for me, and he doesn't want to mess up and give it to the wrong person. "I guess you're still hot for me not coming to your graduation."

"We don't need to talk about that. I'm the same, just older than that picture you lied about."

"Come again?"

"My Razorback football picture." Louisa whispers *no* and flags her hands side to side.

"Get it right, okay? I said Texas A&M," Ed says. He laughs out, a high note not unlike my son's when I pitch him up and catch his fall. "It sounded good then."

"Just look for someone who looks like you. With a wife and a baby."

"Can do," my father says. "On the front lawn. Or was it steps?"

"Of the capitol. Markham Street along the river. You'll see it."

My father says, "I'm here. Tell your wife not to worry. I'll be waiting for you."

"Sounds good. I'll wear a white hat," I throw in for some crazy reason. I don't even own one.

"I love you, Jack."

He waits for a few seconds while I try to think of a reply. Then we hang up on each other, and I almost believe he has learned to mean what he says. Who can tell?

On the way over, I talk Louisa into stopping at a place called Buster's, where I once waited tables and dreamed of making my father myths into something worth telling the truth about. For one whole year I worked the lunch crowds and spent long nights into mornings on *The Book of Lies*.

Finally, I understood why it would never work; to tell a lie, you must know the truth.

We get a table around the time we're supposed to be meeting Ed, and I order two mimosas and some honey for Jack's pacifier. From our window we see the gold dome flare on top of the state capitol building, where my mother has worked for twenty-five years in a ground-floor office. Beside the structure, dark against the green lawn, is the small lake where we used to meet for her lunch hour. We were there on the sunny Tuesday when she said she'd been proposed to and asked what I thought about her getting married to Frank Bottoms. I remember how the goldfish— big as saucers with eyes full of a glitter I associated with meanness—broke water, fighting for a piece of bread, a saltine cracker, or my hand, I guessed, if it was offered.

When I said, "No," my mother did a strange thing. "See this lake," she said, and I remember how she swept her graceful ringless hand across its breadth, "it belongs to you. Never forget that." Years later, I understood that this was *public* property—everyone owned it—but then I honestly believed that my mother had given me something no man could take away.

"See that lake over there, Jackie? It's yours. Don't you forget it," I say to my sleeping son, while Louisa taps her watch face.

"We ought to go now." Louisa touches the arm of my jacket in the kind way she must have picked up from watching her mother or father comfort each other in a scary moment.

I look her the eyes. "You're right," I say, "but tell me. What's going to happen to *us*?"

Louisa does not bother hiding tears. She looks down at the table where pieces of her napkin are torn into strips, and the strips into strips. I watch her decide not to say what I need to hear.

"Your father's waiting on you now," she says to someplace I can't see. "We'll be fine."

"You mean the two of us?"

Louisa nods.

I wonder what's come of turning points—the one lucky break we've waited for? Mr. Rush's twenty slides under a champagne glass, and I adjust my tie, the bright yellow that is clearly wrong. We abandon our table and walk through people waiting under fans in the foyer, anxious to take our places.

As we cross the street where a sign flashes *walk* to the place where my father is wondering where we are, little Jack wakes up and recognizes where we are—or at least I think he does. Sometimes Louisa brings him with her on the afternoons when she picks my mother up from work. I fight the urge to demand an explanation of what they talk about, why my wife feels so close to my mother, or if a comparison has been made between me and Ed.

"You should cherish this," Louisa says, as we circle the long white sidewalk that leads to the multitiered steps that glare in this light. Our shoes tick-tock on the concrete. My stomach sinks. Louisa brushes my hair and then hers with a free hand, then holds the son named for my mother in front of us, as if he's some precious gift for a person we've traveled far to see. Above us, the film of sky is a flat blue no eye could ever hold. Heat rises in wisps from the hot sidewalk in front of the capitol—our destination is blurred. Here is how I make my way toward my father, with all I have to lose or gain on this earth by my side.

"Do you see him?" Louisa asks.

We're near enough. Clear, the faces of families come to breathe the day in, enjoying what is left of summer on blankets stretched across the harsh grass, where mothers and fathers just now call wayward children to partake of what has been prepared. A few homeless people are here, and sons with their fathers are going after the star-eyed goldfish, bedded down in shade pockets.

"Jack? Is he here?"

"I don't know. I've never really seen him before."

"Don't be stupid." Louisa says this in a way that asks something of me I may not have to give. "Keep trying."

The three of us stop in our tracks about fifty paces in front of the steps that reach up to the huge double doors where my mother has gone to work all the days of her adult life. I say, "I'm not sure."

"*God*, let him be here for your sake." Louisa cradles Jack high on her shoulder, and I'm not sure which one of us she's wishing for.

To our left, a small crowd has gathered around the worn chunk of stone Little Rock is named for. Some vandal has splattered red paint on its face, and I wonder if I can find my father there.

"He could be anywhere," I say, and draw my wife and son close. A side of me I can't call by name is pulling loose, inventing, dreaming up why Ed isn't here: he's drunk with an air force buddy in the hotel lobby, he's with my mother—skipping stones on the lake, he was hit by a bus and his heart has just quit beating on an emergency room table. They dial the voltage high for one last shock. A thin voice asks, "Time?"

"What happens now, Jack?"

Then I see him.

His face hangs in a shaft of light near the top step, the fine wrists and small hands I've passed on to my son held to his brow as he searches over all of us who are strangers for the white hat, the wife and child, the son he would make peace with before the grave. Questions go off like pistol shots in my head, but what I feel is not akin to fear or desire for my father. What floors me is a gut sense of shame for what Jack—my baby boy—will know if the day ever comes when he has to call me out to ask why I lied. The Tucson ranch, the motherless little girl, or the promise of a book of lies—they're all the same. And as I see the man my mother left home for and married, I am bewildered by what I miss, how the truth shames.

"He's lost," I hear myself say.

"Are you *sure*?" Louisa fights tears. "Keep looking for him," she says, and shifts our son so he faces my father. Ed is looking straight at our faces now, deciding.

"I think I see him."

"Up there," Louisa says. She ushers my son and me through

many children, up toward the moment, long in coming, where the lie of love is fearless wisdom.

"*Go*," Louisa says, and we leap up two steps at a time for every one my father takes earthward.

DANCE ALL NIGHT

Outside the picture window, beyond the garage, olive-skinned boys piss rainbows off the apartment catwalk, sling Spanish curses down at the spring-crazed dogs. A man named Bruce has just interrupted bacon and eggs to accuse Jack of brainwashing his young wife. Their phone number—Louisa and Jack's—is one digit off the battered women's shelter, downtown. The hot line. Someone's always calling. Most often, before he answers, Jack's afraid his mother has died, that he'll never hear her voice again.

Today. A fine, bright Saturday. "Goddamnit," Bruce says. "Please. Just put her on the phone and let us talk."

"You're a number off," Jack says. "You've got the wrong number."

Bruce tells Jack not to fuck with him. He's knows Jack's name, has seen his pretty wife. "Don't shit me," he says. "Shoot me straight. I'll shoot you straight."

Louisa's quit answering.

"I bought something I want to give her," Bruce says. "Her cat keeps fucking meowing. You can't keep her there."

"Hang up, Jack."

Louisa's in her rose-print pajamas. They've laced their coffee with a little morning whiskey. Maybe they'll thin lettuce later, or walk to the park where fat geese are laying eggs on the pond bank, or turn on bluegrass and drink beer. Maybe, they'll make love. It's that kind of day. Jack misses it, and it isn't even gone, yet.

Louisa forks a yellow hunk of egg, lets it drop. She says, "It's Saturday."

In the background, Jack can hear someone talking, asking for something. Or maybe it's the television. Cartoons.

"Keep my wife out of this. You don't know us."

"Wrong. I know where you're at. Chief. You're right in front of my face."

It occurs to Jack that he's heard this man's voice before, he's sure of it. Jack has never forgotten a voice in his life.

"Let me speak to her. Her cat's sick for Jesus' sake. Tell her her cat's sick."

"No."

"What's with you?" Morning is Louisa's quiet time. They don't really speak until after noon. They've made rules.

"I know I'm a good person. Just like you," Bruce says.

Louisa swipes at the receiver, knocks it onto the table, flipping Jack's coffee mug. Some goes onto the lamp. The bulb pops, hisses.

Jack says, "Goddamnit."

"Don't."

Sometimes, a sliver of time verges between one thing and the next. The two parts touch. Jack's seen it go both ways.

"I'm sorry."

"I know."

Then, in front of their faces, sun shining through, the voice thins high and reedy, says, *I'll knock ever tooth out of your head. I killed her fuckin cat in the bathtub. Watch your ass. Hear? I'll be back.*

Across the drive, the Mexican boys shoot off rounds from small-caliber pistols. Tiny *pops.* Kids, their guns sound like toys. *Pop. Pop, pop.*

He hangs up. Picks up and hangs up again. Louisa and him. They look at each other, then away. Louisa says, "Fuck this."

Watch your ass. *Watch out for me.*

Two rooms away, their toddler works and reworks a floor puzzle.

Jack hears his wife walk the hall, hard words.

Jack and Louisa have planted a backyard garden, an exact replica of the ones they cultivated in North Carolina. Snow peas are up, spinach and spring onion. Louisa's cross-legged in the lettuce, thinning, while Jack shovels up an untilled bed. Three-year-old Jacky hoes strawberry vine with a plastic tool. The wild, woolly dogs chase magpies yard to yard among stunning jonquil and tulip. Out here, packs of them run uncollared. In bed, they hear them fight each other all night, fixing and refixing the old hierarchy under murderous Orion.

"Monday, we're getting a new number." Jack buries the lug, heaves a shovelful. "I've had it."

Louisa's pulling way too much, pinching the green gold leaf in handfuls. To get my goat, Jack thinks.

"They'll find us."

His wife is barefoot. Her feet have always had a look about them. Beat or something. Dancing feet.

"Not if we have a new number."

"I want meat tonight. I want to eat meat," Louisa says.

"What do you mean they'll find us out?"

"Out?" She's destroying beautiful greens, half a row gone, waiting for Jack to say so. "Steaks. Fillets this thick." Black Seeded Simpson flies this way and that.

Randy salsa brava music pours out of the next-door apartments, and Jack smells pork cooking over charcoal. *Carnitas,* small meats, they devour them. Night or day, makes no difference. The boys see everything. Jacky's sentence—*what those boys are doing?*

"Lay off on that lettuce."

"Bloody. Raw's good for bones."

Louisa lives to fight. She gets way into it, Jack believes, would rather fight than fuck—any day of the week. "Crud in your veins. It'll kill you."

"That guy on the phone. *He* needs a heart attack."

Jack says, "Please," and digs away, toward roots, hard pack.

He's good with a shovel, any kind of spade, really. It's in his blood, gets his heart rate up.

"*You* fucking please. Oh Jack, *please, please, please.*"

Bones. Bones break into bones. Jack pictures his father. It was *his* saying. Father and son. He'd said it all the time.

"Please what?" He digs, cuts a maple root—white flesh.

"Anything," Louisa says. "Anything at all."

Tonight is Full Flower Moon. Across the street, on green clover growing in a backyard that matches Jack's, a coven of wiccans is gathering for tonight's drum circle. They look like regular people—a waitress, a baker, a candlestick maker, whatever—but in a while they'd be belly deep in dance, gusto and breasts and hip sway in the milky light, swinging, hands clasped for the castration, the curved knife above the night-green lawn, while the dark-hard Mexican boys waved their penises in mock cry, pissed rainbow arches, and made their own dance above the catwalk's sour concrete.

"Our dogs would have hated it here."

The shovel slices old, rooty loam, hits rock, a stake through the heart. His son has her eyes. *What those boys are doing, Da?* "We don't have dogs."

Louisa says, "If we did. They wouldn't have done well. Not here." She's up now, windmill stretching, sun watering her eyes. "They're better off never having known us."

Jack says, "Go ahead. Talk through it."

She says, "Much better. Don't you think?"

When Louisa walks away from him, tall, sun-gold, her jean shorts ride up new-hard thighs. She's taken up exercise, lately. Jazzercise. Something like that. "Whatever you say."

"I want steak. How's our charcoal?"

"How?"

"Are we out?" She speaks without looking back at him.

Above them, the boys wolf whistle, massage their crotches in full view of their son, who stands staring. Their words connect—

the rolled *r*'s machine-gunned with many meanings. *Medusoid*, Jack thinks.

Louisa flirts with them, outrageously. She dares Jack to see, always.

"Watch out, Louisa."

This second she offers herself to them. With her eyes, fucks them right in front of his face, his son's face.

She says, "Sure, Jack. Bye-bye."

The other morning, a new fawn, white spots and all, lay gutted on their front yard. Belly chewed through. Little Jack riveted— bloody little hooves under the big sky. Right here in the city, Louisa says spring has got into the loose dogs' blood.

That's how Jack feels, now.

Spring in his blood.

Louisa's old boyfriend broke her jaw once. They'd been arguing over his going to bars or failing his accountant exams or playing music too loud at night or something stupid like that. She claims he was drunk. Her story goes like this: one minute he was there, in their kitchen, having the sort of fight they'd had a hundred times, and the next minute he was crazy, throwing hooks. Roundhouses. He bit her chest, pulled hair out, got her in the face a few times, a right cross smacked her cheekbone. After, when she was on the mend, he'd do anything for her, spend his money, cook supper, do the laundry, clean the toilet, eat shit, anything.

Jack met the guy once, at an outdoor concert, the blues. Louisa'd asked for a beer, and Jack had stood in line for forty minutes. When he made it back, Jack found the two of them talking, this guy and Louisa about to argue.

Louisa introduced them, and Jack offered to shake.

"Just wait," the old boyfriend said, "this one's a bitch."

Jack'd said, "What?" He handed Louisa both beers.

The guy smirked. "A bitch."

What do you say? Fight fast? Surprise the opponent?

Even when glass was broken or letters burned, their rows were nothing compared to broken jaws. No. Not even the worst. Not even with the kid watching. Nothing like broken bones.

By the time Louisa makes it home, Jack's turned over every unplanted foot in the plot. Shovel deep, the blue dirt shines up to the hedge line where the old tenant's yellow rose has root rot. The blight, Jack thinks. It's happy hour. Jack's thirsty. He's poring over his options for getting high. Little Jack's asleep on the grass. Red wine. What's left of the bourbon. 7-11 beer. The Mexican boys are full throttle now, onto the witches, calling them bitch, cocksucker, cunt, *puta. ¡la muy puta!* Jack knows *puta.*

Louisa slams the truck door. Already, it seems, she's screaming. From the garden where he huffs, the garage door is invisible. But he hears his wife's voice, the mean one reserved only for him in this universe.

She's enlisted the Mexicans against him. He hears their voices, their banter, their lusty threats.

What the fuck. Give her what she wants.

He's thinking it as he walks to meet them, shovel hefted over a shoulder. He's good with a spade. In his head, he sees it swing, hears the sound, sees the old shock on both of their faces.

What's gotten into him? Spring in his blood.

This is the way it happens. Tiny blood vessels go off, metallic, sparking.

Jack stomps around the corner. He sees it coming.

Half in his drive and half on his street, a truck with a lopsided metal rack is running, missing on a cylinder. Something's wrong with the hood and bumper. Jack can't put his finger on what. A man Jack's seen before walks toward them from the backside of the house. Just walks on out from a piss. He's zipping his pants, neither smiling nor frowning. He says, "Told you I'd be around."

Louisa's behind their truck's tailgate, just standing there blank faced. A plastic grocer's bag balloons at her feet. A box of croutons, one fat rib eye have fallen out.

Above them, the Mexicans have faces like many moons before an eclipse, any second about to disappear. A long way off, the boy.

Louisa says, *"Jack."*

This familiar man nods. He's Jack's height. He grins. Jack grins back. Louisa bends over, grasps the crouton box, is saying that the son of a bitch has followed her. Two, three seconds. That's all.

Jack says, "Excuse me?"

While he says it, the other makes a fist. At his side. Finger by finger. His uppercut gets Louisa.

In the face.

That sound. She's confused. Blood comes in one nostril. In the corner of her eye. She's reaching for the croutons, still, when he gets her again.

Again, the unforgettable sound of it.

Our fights are nothing like this.

Jack says, "*Stop—don't.*"

Now Louisa recognizes. Knows. The second one hurts. She'll show all week.

In the drive, the truck dies. The Mexicans are back. They never went away. Out in the yard, the boy sits up, sees.

Jack is half swing. A shovel blade is blue and white. A split tenth of a second. The other leans away. Backward. Eyes lifted upward, toward the catwalk. Light blue, his eyes. Pieces of sky. Louisa starts a scream. Just the beginning of one.

When he was ten, in Arkansas, on Shelly Street, Jack got into a backyard fistfight with a twelve-year-old named Ricky O'Neil. O. W., Jack's stepfather, watched. O'Neil tore his shoes off, his socks. Silent, everything was quiet and that otherworldly feel of being hit in the face. It doesn't hurt, not at all, really. But it's quite surprising—very much so. And that's what Jack was, surprised by his lips, his eyes, his nose and ears, that they be numb that way. When it was over, Jack shivering under sheets, his stepfather, his old man, his keeper, walked in with a dirty shoe in each hand. He threw one, a fat *thwack* against the far wall. The other. *How could you let that sissyshit win?* Then his father walked out, and that was that.

Louisa, full bloom in his ear. It was all her.

The shovel in dead air. It spins Jack around, misses. Why is this happening?

Pistol fire glares up on the catwalk, light before sound, just like that. Out of the sky. Forget slow motion. It's not like that at all. A pink streak glazes the forehead of the guy who hit Louisa.

This guy—Bruce from breakfast?—touches his eyebrow with

his fingers. He says, "Shit, man" and "don't you do that again." Head blood is darker than the rest.

Louisa's face blooms that crazy shade, not blue, not purple.

Cop cars come. They know this area, have been here. One has a pump shotgun—a twelve. Another a rifle. Everyone save Jack and Louisa has a gun pointed at somebody.

The shot man climbs up onto Jack and Louisa's roof. Like a monkey, the cops say. By then, a television crew is there, rolling. The guy takes his shoes off—brown, dog-licked-looking things. He throws his cheap shoes one at a time at the cops. The television crew believes they can make hay out of this, catching a shot man bleeding and throwing his shoes. "Give us more," they say before it's over. The Mexicans claim that they can't speak English, none of them knows a word. *Nada.*

The cops make Jack and Louisa file a report. Write things down on paper. Louisa doesn't seem mad, now. They've each got a cup of wine and are out by the driveway, where the white truck still sits.

Jack and Louisa take the cop with the notebook through their day. It's too late to start charcoal. They'll have to use the oven. In the living room, little Jack's white face behind the plate-glass window.

Louisa says, "I'm real hungry. We want to eat."

But the cop asks for more. "Did he hit you with his fist or his hand?" he asks. "It makes a difference."

Louisa tells him again. The cop scribbles. His handwriting, Jack notices, is childish scrawl. Bird track.

"Once or twice. We need to get this straight."

"Twice," Louisa says.

"In the face, right? You said he hit you in the face. I can't tell."

Louisa steps back. Framed behind her, Jack sees his son, attention trained on the bevy of women across the street come to dance under a full moon.

"With his hand," Louisa says. "Like this. In a fist. Got it. You want some more?" She shows him again, shows him the steps.

Ice would help that swelling.

"One more time. Why? What did you do to him? You flip him off, or what?"

Neighbors go on as if nothing has happened. Over there, Mack, whose name is Jack but whose lisp makes it come out "Mack," still doesn't care two damns which you call him. The Mexicans. The afternoon has run off and left them. Shadows really are long. Hungry people are carving up chickens, fat roasters, save the witches. Just now, Jack sees, they're erecting the dance pole, its phallus head painted Aristotle red—flared as fish gill. Colorful ribbons get into the wind, snap circles in the light air. Across the street, the women orbit each other. They lay the rock circle, gather scraps to burn. Strange to Jack, they blur, are gashes of bright green cloth, skin skeining from bone. A few hurdle stretch in the grass. One brushes another's long black hair, laces bits of green gold leaf into its twisted length. Jack's tired. He's not a bad man.

"Tell me how it started? I need a reason here."

Blood clots one nostril. It's still there. "Ask *him*," Louisa says. "Tell this prick how it started, Jack."

Louisa says this and walks away. Just turns and walks, down the drive, around the back of the house. Jack hears the storm door shut.

She's gone.

And he is speechless in front of the lawman. He can't think of a single word. Not one.

Across the street, they've circled. Around and around the fire's pink licks, under a moon named for flowers, the women dance.

Louisa takes a hot bath in the dark, while Jack readies the meat, potatoes, button mushrooms, a curt daffodil to lay beside his wife's rare fillet. Her face is not so bad, not so bad at all, Jack thinks. It could have been worse. Something could have been broken—teeth, or her nose, even. The worst is when it shows. When she has to walk around that way saying, I ran into a wall, or I wrecked my ten-speed, I fell downstairs. Sunglasses. Cover stick that never covers.

It had all happened so quickly.

Faced with the same thing again, the running truck, the man zipping his pants, approaching, Jack wouldn't hesitate. He'd take the man out, knock every tooth out of *his* head. Break his bones into bones.

From the tub, Louisa says, "More wine," and Jack takes her another cupful of red. Gives it to where her voice says, "Here." At night, she bathes in the dark. It relaxes her, she says.

"Wash your back?"

She says, "Where's Jacky?"

"Asleep."

"He's okay? No dreams?"

"Sure."

Jack lathers the cloth, feels his way to Louisa's neck, works his way down her shoulder blades, wide for a woman and hard muscle, to the base of her back, where a bulging vertebra hurts when weather's coming. Some of the moon leaks in through the rolled-shut window. He can hear her breathing, the sound her feet make in the hot water. Sightless, Jack smells his wife's skin, the sweet odor she makes in the water.

"I wish it was me instead of you."

"Was or were? I'm starving."

Jack says it again, hears water heave and roll, and leaves her in the dark.

They eat on a tablecloth folded in half on the bedroom floor. The sound no longer works on their television, but they turn it on anyway. Tonight is an opera—*Tosca*—and they tune in during a vale of tears. Something terrible has happened. The woman lead has real tears running, no, gushing, Jack sees, down her face. He wishes that he could hear her voice, know what she is saying because it looks like it's important. Life or death.

Louisa is cross-legged. She's digging in, going to town. She's bought thick fillets, three, four fingers, maybe. She only eats rare. Blood has leaked into the sour cream that has slid off her baked potato.

They've started a second bottle of cabernet.

"Jack?" She saws through a thick slice of beef and takes it, dripping between the thumb and index finger of her left hand, up to her face. "What do you think's into her? What's happened?"

"Who knows?"

The woman singer could be attractive. Her face is red, and the veins on her neck have gone purple. Maybe she has children somewhere, watching her cry; probably, they want to help, but can't. Her counterpart is tall and husky. He tries to make her stop crying, but she refuses. "I don't know," Jack says, again. "She's got a problem."

Louisa presses the slice of meat against her swollen left eye, holds it there, and begins to munch bits of the stuffing from inside her potato, croutons, and Bacos. "I know, but guess. Take a wild guess."

On screen, the woman lies down, rakes her forearm over her face. "Maybe she's dying."

Louisa retrieves the meat from her eye, puts it in her mouth, chews, and swallows. "Let's try. One more time."

Before Jack knows it, she's on her feet in front of the dresser and the mute television. A bloody rivulet runs down her chin, her neck.

Outside, across the street, Jack can hear the women making noisy dance. One wolf howls. Jack swears.

"What are you doing?"

But Louisa has opened her right hand wide, down by her hip. "*Take it, bitch,*" she says and slaps the set hard on its side, once, and then again. It spits for a second or so. She says, "You want some fucking more?" and casts Jack a thin smile.

Then, full blare, the sound is on them, barreling down the hall toward their son. They hear what they've been missing.

Later, in bed, they can make out the ruckus going on outside, building and waning, quitting and starting. Jack's arm is falling asleep under Louisa's back, but he doesn't want to move. He just wants to keep things still. He thinks she's asleep.

It's not dark enough with the moon out like this. Pieces of his life fly by: somewhere, way off, he hears his mother through a sheetrock wall, asking, *pleading* for him to go get help, anybody. "He's killing me," she says. "The son of a bitch is *hurting* me." He pictures it, how he pictured it then, real fists caving in the old man's skull. He had grown up loving angry women. Maybe it had gotten inside him, like spring got into dogs. He's not a bad man. He's never broken bones.

"Jack. Are you awake?"

"Yes."

"I want to, Jack. Let's do it, now."

So they start. Her on top. Out the cracked blinds, Jack sees the strange women, caught up under the full-moon dance. On tiptoes, their feet barely touch.

Spring is on them. They've made it through their first Utah winter. They'll be okay. They'll make it. Jack hopes. They will always be okay.

Louisa says, "I love you."

Jack is pushed into her. Louisa settles the last bit. The motion, the old rocking, made and repeated.

Again and again. Jack remembers how a woman that year, caught in the high country during a horrendous April blizzard, had managed to survive an entire night alone by dancing. He and Louisa, they've witnessed those storms, how they roar in over the big salt lake and blow everything to kingdom come. But this woman lived to tell—it was miraculous, but true. She heard this music, this jazzing in her head. Hour after hour after hour, she tromped circles in a gale-force wind, powder drifts high as housetops. Against all earthly odds, against exposure, frostbite, hypothermia, dehydration, convulsions, demoralization—all infirmities of the flesh and spirit, she danced all night. With music existing solely in her head, she lived to tell. A ski patrol found her in the morning, frostbit and exhausted, dancing. Later, a news crew interviewed her from her hospital bed. She knew that she could make it, this woman said, if she just kept dancing. *What on earth?*

"All I want," Louisa is saying.

They breathe into each other's faces.

Outside, Jack hears the souls of the damned, bleating, begging for mercy. He says, "Tell me."

THE LIFETIME LONELINESS SCALE

It happened during an afternoon before it rained, when the air smelled like nothing but the way air smells before it rains. She came coasting into his drive—a beat old station wagon with a wrinkled driver's fender. Right in front of his house, the wheels quit turning. She got out, looked at the car the way you look at a thing that's way past empty, then up at his front door. She didn't resemble anybody he knew, was someone who would have been chosen to play the movie part of what was just then happening— pretty, lank tall, wearing a short, beige waitress uniform with some writing sewn tongue colored into the heart side. He hasn't forgotten that, the pink writing. The sun was fierce—you don't know unless you've been here—and her eyes were naked, nothing was covering the bright white in her Mormon-blue eyes. She had a lover, a husband maybe. He was sure of this. She looked that way. He'd be thin, believe himself dangerous, take her on moody drives after dark, make fierce faces in all three mirrors.

She opened the hood. He watched her for a minute through the bedroom window before unbuttoning the second shirt button, swiping at his hair and walking out. "Can I help you?" he asked.

"Can you," she said. "I don't know."

He doesn't remember that her voice was striking, but it must have been. I'll say it was.

The engine was big, a v-8, an oil burner, and she'd already screwed off the breather nut. Grime had got under her nails. She wore her wristwatch face down.

"Let me look at it," he said.

She smelled good, of faith and shampoo. She said, "Fuck."

"Excuse me?"

She said, "I'm out of gas. It's happened before."

He told her that he would be right back and on the way to get the mower can thought about "fuck," how the word sounded on her tongue. Louisa, his wife, had written m-o-w-e-r in big black letters from a permanent marker to distinguish the gas can from its look-alike weed-eater mate. Now, the mower can was nearly empty, a cupful at the most.

"I'm out," he said. "You take this can if you like. I'd take you. My car's out of whack."

This time she mouthed the word. The hard k made a tiny sucking sound against the roof of her mouth. Then the small smile, and she took the red gas can out of his hands and started walking downhill, and he watched her walk away for a long time.

In the movie, the one his head makes, she would have turned her head back midstride, said something, maybe, hip sway turning the blond, blond heads of passersby. And that's exactly what she does. Down to the randy toss-back of her honeyswirl hair—it was the color of burnt light. He would be a good person come on hard times, salt of the earth loading a pawnshop pistol.

"Shut the fuck up," he said to a dog across the street. A writer friend was always saying that dogs barking were so cliché, not at all acceptable in the world of truth, which, he'd learned, meant the world of lies.

He said, "How long does it take to fall out of love?" and threw a crushed beer can, more barking. "Babies bark backward in the bucolic bay of night." Write it down, he thought.

They lived in Utah. No hallucinative stretch of the imagination could ever prepare you for the shock of seeing a hundred miles off your own front porch. Turn your head the other way, a hundred more. The eye filled up by the world's sooty-red curve, copper mine, smokestack and the letter *C,* Nevada way off. The mountains on the east and west sides of the valley had snow on them year round. It went ruby gold at dawn and dusk. Spring was a harsh beauty—tulips gushing red and yellow and white in the crisp, cold, heavy-particulated air.

Women who loved women who loved men mowed grass in spring snowstorms, the wheels making little grassy tracks across their white, white yards.

Once, an elderly neighbor woman was shearing purple blooms off the tall pussy willow across the street, readying it for a real storm. He heard her shriek. He guessed that she'd fallen off the stool, gashed the side of her face with a shear blade. Outside, he watched the fingers unfold from her cheek, one at a time as if adding the times she'd seen comets or exposing a gift (in a film, unfolding fingers are just fingers). Inside the retirement home, he called her ancient husband from the basement room where he slept. He wheezed behind the lower door, just wheezing—ripped sandpaper—for a few seconds before it swung open.

The old man's robe was an exact match of his, flannel, black and red, a little faded. "What t' hell you want me to do about it?" he asked.

"Your wife," he said. "She's bleeding out on the sidewalk. I'm calling."

"Goddamnit," he said, "I'm seventy-eight years old."

Outside, the woman—the lady he and Louisa called Winter because that's when they'd first seen her face behind a window— was gone. He traced dark head blood across the outside walk, up into the outer door and into a kitchen, where now she was bleeding into the sink. He used the phone. Five minutes had passed.

The EMTs, a caterwauling fire truck, then a police car and an ambulance. The old man seemed yellow now, old, yelling out his age, his birthday, his first wife's secret name—which only he knew because it was solemnized in the Temple, which was always just called the Temple. People milled outside, in their hands whatever they'd been doing at the time: a letter, a paring knife, a still baby with carrot hair, nothing.

This would always be in his head: the bleated cry, the crouched body, the fingers opening one at a time, the old man, the dark door opening. The rest.

Or consider the story about a man who'd been in a plane crash on his way home from work, how the commuter airplane landed in a golden field by a barn on a rainy spring day. No one was killed. The people were whisked into town on school buses, where they in turn boarded subways and made their ways home, less than an hour late in all. But this guy, the man in the story, felt like the plane wreck was profound, like it was somehow a turning point in his life. He walked in the front door of his suburban house as Saul of Tarsus might have the day his eyes peeled. His three children were having their daily squabble. They wouldn't listen. And his wife—she no longer desired to be desired for what she found in mirrors—had lit the candelabra, was serving out chicken Dijon or something on wild rice, and she wouldn't listen. It didn't make a dent, his story about crashing in a plane that afternoon.

Later that evening, at the tail end of the whoever's suburban party they'd been invited to drink martinis at, this guy who'd been in a plane crash, who was well off with a nice house, wife, and family, left by himself. He drove home, unlocked his front door, and molested the baby-sitter—stuck his tongue in her mouth. Out of the clear blue sky.

He'd tried to tell Louisa. He tried, for all he was worth, to make her see the significance. How it happened.

And against that backdrop of that sky, across the certain realism of distance, he saw the pretty woman coming, struggling gracefully up the steep hill. Toward him.

Behind the back bumper, he watched her telescope the plastic funnel into the tank hole, some spilling into oily spots on her white work shoes. Gas—he loved the smell, the sound, *gasoline*. "Is that your name? On your blouse?"

A horse pissing into a metal bucket, maybe that's what could approach the sound of pouring gas into the tank of a station wagon in the afternoon flowering before a rain.

"I wish," she said. Her fingers touched the delicate pink threads above her breast. "I like it. But it's definitely not mine. It should be somebody's."

"Lyra?"

"She's not me."

Lightning has a color all its own, a way to the northwest—directions, in a big space, mean something—over the big Antelope Island. He said, "I don't understand."

"I wear this blouse to work. Lyra's a fake name. It's a constellation. We don't tell customers our real names."

"Customers?"

"Patrons. People we serve."

He said, "*Hey.*"

"What."

"Save some. To prime."

"I know. This's happened before."

She squatted. In front of him that sound. Before it rains the air tastes moist because this was the desert, where every dry-shrunken H_2O-starved board in every house on every street for five hundred miles was now swelling. You could hear the world creak down to cabinet screws, door bolts, floor joists when wet air came. Doors refused closings until summer.

She said, "Here. Go ahead," and sat down into the dark front seat. "Keep your fingers crossed."

Through the crack between the hood and windshield, he motioned for her to go ahead, dripped some down into the breather cover, where he forced the carburetor's metal lip open. The ignition turned over. Four high-pitched turns. He's aware of the belts, the sharp fan.

In the movie, the car never starts. They try everything they can think of until the battery goes dead and no one passing or parked across the street at the retirement home—there, the elderly often jumped off the ninth floor in their Sunday suits, wigs, and holy undergarments—has jumper cables. He invites her inside, and she says *water* and *¿dónde está su baño?* She goes loudly, then uses the phone, and no one is answering.

He starts to show her things: the shadowy spot across the street where Winter fell, a framed diploma, Louisa's flute, the basement where a map of the celestial universe is tacked up on the ceiling of a room with nothing in it. She lies down on cement in the bare light. They seek the whale, the dragon, Pollux and Castor, major and minor dogs, but Lyra escapes them because some of Sagittarius is missing.

"That's funny," she says. "Something's always missing. You think we're really even here now? Is this happening?"

He is with her on the cement where bare light drains in from a broken window. Maybe her blouse is falling open from the third button and she sees him see the hint of areola, and it doesn't matter. She has not shaved her underarms today, or yesterday, or last month.

Before, maybe he tells her about how Napoleon used to write Josephine from four days out. Don't bathe, he would tell her, and she wouldn't for the four days until he came. She let herself grow strong. Of filth and shampoo, cement grit, and himself, he would recall how what happened happened in faint light leaking into the clear, colorful universe where Lyra was missing.

On the next try, as the ignition bumped over a fifth time, the motor hit, caught, and fired. A hard miss. She rolled her window farther down. It was raining big wonderful rain by then.

"Thank you, Mister Mower," she said.

He looked at her, honestly confused.

She pointed to the can at his feet. MOWER, in big black letters, Louisa had written. Then she pointed to her breast where pink *Lyra* was written, grinned, and rolled back out into the slow traffic that took her. Sweet water gushed in the gutters.

Across the street, white through the glass, old Winter's face tilted behind a glass pane. Her eyes were the green of growing things. She'd seen. He saw it register, the pink scar laced into the paper skin. She watched him see her from the street of gasoline rainbows.

He was wet and she was Winter, laughing, and the complete

sky rained down rain in his face, and he did not wish to ever move forever.

Louisa would be home soon, little Jack in tow. No crash, she'd birth a second child. January snow—in view of a frozen fountain where seagulls flew knurls and old men threw bread to the wind.

Lyra, for clustered stars, a girl named Lyra for stars.

We always fight for our lives, shedding light.

WHERE WORDS GO

I'm a word man, can start anywhere. Monday. Three o'clock sun shreds the unspeakable trees. Outside, where snow humps in patches, men who grew up loving angry women walk heavy under the chain-link sheen. My students today, nine, they circle the cinder-block room. I make ten. Three sex crimes steer clear, look at their feet, know stories but are Jesus freaks now and won't tell. The thieves stare at these, see open game. I've been warned. One, Celestino Gaza, vehicular homicide, carves his dry forearm with a thick-ridged thumbnail, he's ex-Marine, is carving a penis, a flower, himself. To him, I'm nobody he wants around. I wish for ripe gold light, slant through blackjack oak in Arkansas autumn, persimmon chilled sweet in frosty air, blacksnake sliced into alfalfa bales fallen in elysian pastures, I tell them, my inmate writers, about my brother, Jimmy.

"He was a stutterer," I say. "Have I told you this?"

Ray, bright-eyed molester, has me nailed, stiffens for the lie of how we all overcome handicaps. Dark Gaza bench-presses 305, a guard watches him through the door window. The wall clock ticks. Pencils and paper are holy.

"Why I'm telling you this is because you've got to figure out your hot spots. You got to know what *means* something to you. Anyone played poker with toothpicks?" The air we breathe seems breathed already, fake air, airplane air. The god with the big stick has walked out, but you can still smell him.

They nod. We talk poker. Five card, seven card, Mexican sweat, the jack with one eye. All decks are marked here, stacked time. "But why won't toothpicks work?"

"Ain't no bet." Ray's voice sounds nothing at all of cigarettes, of urgency whispered under low lights.

"That's the truth. What's on the line?"

Sometimes you can *see* them go home in their heads. Gaza's arm leaks a tiny thread of blood. He makes letters, a cross. The still room has a feel, a velocity.

"Jimmy stuttered. He was eighteen. That makes me twenty-four. The year I cured him."

All my life I've heard about here, a man with a tattoo on his ass—*abandon all hope ye who enter here.*

"It's August. Arkansas. I'm from Arkansas. We drive up Cut Hill, a mile top to bottom. The highest place we can find. And there's a God sign on top that says *Prepare to meet God,* and Jimmy and I piss there. We've brought beer, a case or something. Bud. It's not the first time. Alcohol is forbidden in my family. It made my old man crazy if he knew we boozed. He's recovering. Recovering whores, pious bitches."

Ray winces, a reformed whore, sodomy, buggery, love misguided.

"Jimmy's driving because I've lost my license. D.W.I. number five. Felony. It's dark, and we're out in the country, that country-ass smell when dew hits the bitterweed. Someone has thrown a gutted gar on the side of the road. We can smell it but don't care. We drink and don't talk, under a sky where Jupiter's just come out. My brother and me."

"Can I say something?" A thief whose name I can't put my finger on raises his hand.

The rule is that we don't raise hands. I believe in interruption; my religion.

"No." My session is after lunch, kill time. "Jimmy cut a hole in his and shotgunned it. Two, three, we'd drink like that. You know what I mean?"

A long time without liquor, they almost smile. The guard in the ugly window hates it when you smile. His stick is so beat up it seems real. What ta fuck you grinning at? he'll ask you.

"Jimmy starts his truck. We're high by then. He guns it, keeps the lights off. And we drive down Cut Mountain full throttle in the dark. We don't talk about it. And we don't turn the radio on. It's all my idea, so I make the rules. No talking allowed on the way down. Piss your pants, fine, but no talk. And when we get to the bottom, I don't know why, I couldn't tell you with a gun to my head, doesn't matter, because he could talk then, open up and let fly, read road signs, anything. He didn't miss a lick. We'd go out, dance with air force women. Jimmy quit stuttering. It worked."

Gaza says, "Big shit." All men wish to seem dangerous. If you can't inspire love, fear.

"My daddy set me on fire wunst." Ray pulls up the front of his blue issue; exquisite welts twist across his skinny, sunk-in chest. "Guess that qualifies as a hot spot. Lay money again that."

It's Wednesday, we meet three days a week when they let us. Six of us today, we're losing weight. Tino to my left this time, never sits the same spot twice. Our guard's chewing on a ham biscuit, his jaws saw just outside the door window.

"Shoot," I say.

"Some of it's a lie. You said that's okay."

We are allotted half-hour slots for our workshop sessions. To-day, it's me, Tino, Ray, a small-time called Two Chicken, and an-other fellow I have trouble placing because he neither talks nor moves. God makes six. "That's why we're all here. To lie."

"The winter my old man burned our clothes on a fireplace grate. Just like that. Come home and instead of being ass drunk he's straight sober. Our electricity was shut off that January, so we had a fire going in the fireplace and had burned a quarter mile of wood fence all the way to the curve in the road where the sway-back horse was buried. Come walking in. Just walk on into the living room."

Ray's eyes go aflutter; he's a believer gone home. Nobody in here says *bighouse*.

"Right past my mother and duddn't say a word, not to me, not to my sister, not to the goddamn dog, not to nobody. Nothing, not even a funny look in his eyes. He was just home, hungry probably. And then he comes walking right back in with an armload of my mama's clothes from her closet, drops them on the fire. She ast him why he was burning her clothes on the wood fire. He said, 'Pray,' and went back for some of mine. 'Happy birthday,' he'd say, or 'Merry goddamn Christmas,' and let fly with a can of lighter fluid. Our dog was biting a hole through the back door, gnawing nails, bolt plate, her name was Suzie. My mother's chiffon robe, and the yellow ducks on my brother's pajamas, and my cowboy shirt, some handkerchiefs, the heel kept falling off one of his boots. He was crazy for that fire, glowing like that. Behind me, my mother said I had to go start the car, point it toward the highway. But before I did it he squirted me, and I still don't know why he dit tat, he'd never done 'at before so why'd . . ."

"You said the fire was already burning." The nameless sex offender, Ray's kin, coming at someone's sister from behind, six-inch blade honed for an hour by the clock until it shaves hair. Jesus forgives, my ass. "Why's he need lighter fluid if the fire's burning?"

"Shut up. He dit it then. I burnt good. Bright sparks, little pieces of fire, I saw it snowing up out the chimney while she ran out the front door saying for me to drive that car, and I did. My first time behind the wheel spewing gravel and smell of my skin where the lighter fluid had caught. Look, goddamnit. Right here. I could smell myself in my own nose. What do you think? What do you think? You tell me what you think it smells like, your own skin in your nose. Out on the highway I rolled my window down. 'Son of a bitch, son of a bitch,' I screamed it in the air, and I remember because the air felt good and saying 'son of a bitch' felt good. My mama kept saying, 'Don't. Just drive,' she said."

"What'd it smell like?"

"Ain't none of it true. It's a goddamn lie." Ray is the shortest man in the room, five-two or something. His eyes blink.

"What's 'at got to do with why you're here. What you did?" Tino's voice reminds me of someone I heard talking from a pulpit once, it livens the air, has a grain to it. Even though I've never heard a smart word come out of his mouth. "Maybe we set you on fire again it'll fix you right."

"It ain't got nothin, Gaza, to do with nothin."

The guard—is his name Wellar?—pushes the door open, we're out of time. I say, "Go and do likewise."

Friday morning is Visiting, so everyone's all screwed up by the time we meet. Have I told you it's winter, that the light out here is different, that I've left a lot of places behind and it always takes so long to leave? Tino chooses a metal chair dead in front of me today; his eyes are brown for what it's worth. Maybe being an ex-Marine Latino postal worker is tough, maybe we should grieve our cowardice, our failed nerve. We both know he'll talk today.

Instructors who work at prisons must first pass tests: the silence between me and Tino gets louder every day, the cells in my body anger, no, rage him, I can feel it happen, proton by proton. I am not a nonstrategic person. "Tino," I say. "Is there anything going on in the world we need to know about today?"

Ray's still pissed about Tino's saying he should set him on fire again. His sideways chair breaks our circle, a face that speaks weary glower, hair and twitch. He won't tell us what it smelled like. When he was on fire.

They ask you how you react to danger; are you or have you ever been a felon or a homosexual or a multiple gun owner? Are you wanted? Are you the victim of abuse? Do you ordinarily feel angry for no reason? Are you an alcoholic or a drug addict, or have you ever been any of these? Have you or any members of your family been in a facility of any kind? Are you bothered by long periods of silence? Are you an alien?

Tino. Still visible, the carved name, the penis, the flower. I say, "I guess nothing in the world."

I've decided to tell another story: one aimed at, rather than understanding one's hot spots, unearthing the power of words, where they go, how they are living and dead, at once freemen and slaves. They cost no money, can go through doors. Shit like that. Tino beats me to the punch.

"I'm not what you say," he says.

Today, we are down to four: myself, Tino, Ray, and the nameless molester, or is he a thief? Doesn't matter. Out in the world, he could be standing at a flea market and his name would be George something, and what would it matter? Who'd care? People are everywhere.

"Say?" Not only are his eyes brown, they have yellow in them, shiny flecks.

"That story about your brother. You turned him into a stutterer. Why?"

It is not a question whose answer rockets through my head.

The testers ask you your philosophy of criminal punishment, how you would explain incarceration to someone for whom the concept did not exist.

"Why is so much at stake in that? What's the bet in telling us about your brother stuttering? Or drinking beer? Driving a truck down a hill? Air force women? What are you about?"

"You killed someone, Tino. Put them in a grave. What are *you* about?" I've been warned.

Tino has good posture, rare. His skin is the color of unbleached olives. "Not talking about me," he says. "We're talking about you."

Ray and the nameless man pass a hand signal. If moments actually verge between one instant and the next, that's what I sense, energy becoming. I say, "Tell me a story, Tino."

He says, "You."

Jimmy, out of my mouth. "That's where they found him," I say.

"The bottom of that hill. Where I used to take him. He went through glass. I found his brains on a tree stump. My cure."

Tino yawns. "You ain't got no monopoly on car wrecks. And the world don't owe you no pat on the back. Got me?"

The door is opening inward. The guard's stick clack-thuds on hardwood.

Ray says, "It smelled like me. It must have *been* me."

The man whose name I don't know pats the slender pad inside the shoulder of the black coat I'm wearing and walks out, followed by Ray. Tino's last. On his way by he drops a paper wad, tight balled, onto my lap. Alone in the cinder-block room, I undo it, and see. I can leave now, drive on out, hit a bar, whatever. I can go home anytime I want.